# SNORRI

## THE AFTERLIFE ADVENTURES OF SNORRI STURLUSON

### BY CHRISTOPHER ALAN SMITH

Copyright © 2024 by Christopher Alan Smith. All rights reserved. This work is not to be reproduced in any form without express written permission of the author.

ISBN: 9781446142783

*This book is dedicated to the immortal memory of Snorri Sturluson, whose works have immeasurably enriched our knowledge of the ancient lore of the Scandinavian peoples.*

# Contents

Acknowledgements ............................................................ 5
Introduction ..................................................................... 6
Chapter 1 - Hel ................................................................. 8
Chapter 2 - Svartálfheim ................................................ 12
Chapter 3 - Vanaheim ..................................................... 28
Chapter 4 - Ljósálfheim .................................................. 42
Chapter 5 – A magical interlude ..................................... 50
Chapter 6 – Muspelsheim ............................................... 55
Chapter 7 – Midgard ....................................................... 62
Chapter 8 – Niflheim ....................................................... 72
Chapter 9 - Jökulheið ..................................................... 85
Chapter 10 - Asgard ....................................................... 98
Chapter 11 - Valhalla ..................................................... 112
Chapter 12 – A Reunion ................................................ 118
Chapter 13 – Mimir's Well ............................................. 130
Chapter 14 - Explanations ............................................. 145
Chapter 15 – Jötunheim ................................................ 153
Chapter 16 - Hrokkvir .................................................... 175

# Acknowledgements

I wish to thank all those who have given me their kind encouragement in the production of this book, including Jason Heppenstall, Mark Patton, Ian Read and, last but not least, my loving wife Laurie. I also thank Michael Kelly for his assistance in producing the cover image.

# Introduction

Who does not love a good tale drawn from Norse mythology? Tales of Odin, the cunning, one-eyed god of poetry, magic and war, ever scheming to avert Raganarök, the twilight of the gods. Tales of the hulking god Thor who, with his mighty hammer Miolnir, battles with the giants. Or of Freya, Tyr, or the trickster-god Loki. From the 19th Century onward, such tales have been popularised in the western world, giving rise to entire genres of music and fiction, from Wagner's operatic ring cycle to Tolkien's 'The Lord of the Rings' trilogy, and to an entire series of Marvel films based on the adventures of Thor. The Vikings and their gods have experienced an enormous resurgence of interest in the 21st Century.

But have you ever asked yourself where these tales come from? Were they always with us? Who wrote them down? Few, as they read the books or watch the films, ponder these questions. When we do look for original sources, we learn that a few fragments are recorded here and there by some dusty old Christian cleric, or in a proscriptive law, or in an isolated folk-tale. The vast bulk, however, of what we know about the old, heathen gods was entrusted to us, down the ages, by one man: Snorri Sturluson.
Snorri Sturluson (1179-1241 CE) was an Icelander. He was born to a wealthy family – one might term it 'baronial' or 'aristocratic' in our modern language – and he had the benefit of an excellent education. In addition to his native language of Old Norse, he learned Latin and had access to oral and written histories. Snorri became a land-owner in mediaeval Iceland, with vast estates. Unfortunately for him, in a half-century of civil war, he was no great warrior-leader. After encountering reverses, he fled to the court of the King of Norway, where he was given high office and esteem. Eventually, however, when he had enough of the King's control, he fled back to Iceland and tried to regain the power that he had previously held. The Norwegian King's displeasure followed him and, in 1241, he was assassinated; some say in his cellar, others say in his bathroom.

But it is not for his land-holdings or political career that Snorri is remembered. His main achievement, as far as we are concerned today, was to write about the old heathen beliefs of the Scandinavian peoples and, by inference, of all pre-Christian Germanic nations. Without Snorri's main writings, the 'Prose Edda' and the 'Heimskringla', we would be very much the poorer. He was undoubtedly a Christian by upbringing but, in his prose, he evinces such a fascination, bordering on admiration, of the old gods that one might imagine him to be a 'closet-Heathen' at a time when that could be dangerous to a person's health. Indeed, one story suggests that his father was a secret devotee of Odin.

Where did Snorri's soul go after his violent death? If he were truly a Christian, it may have gone to the Heaven or Hell of that religion. But if Snorri was, in his heart of hearts, a Heathen... what then? And what if those ancient, Heathen gods had taken notice of his life and writings... noticing errors which needed to be corrected? This story begins with the moment of Snorri's death and takes him on a mystical, magical and often dangerous journey into the afterlife, where he meets with denizens of the nine worlds of Yggdrasil, the world-tree. This book is by no means meant to be a guide to Norse mythology, but it is inspired by the old lore recorded by Snorri in the *'Gylfaginning'* section of his Prose Edda. It is a fantasy, and I hope you will enjoy it.

# Chapter 1 - Hel

As his assassins stood back, their swords dripping blood, Snorri Sturluson sank to his knees, eyes vacant. His last thoughts were that he was dying, unshriven, with no priest to hear his confession, and that his servants would grumble at having to clean up all this blood in the bathroom. Then he was falling, and none of it seemed to matter anymore.

He fell for a long time, a cacophony of disjointed sounds, voices and images entering his mind, as they do when one is falling asleep after a busy day. A man juggled with knives, seven in the air at any one time. "Ask him his name yourself!", said the man, and disappeared. "Jafnhárr… hárr… hárr… hárr" another voice echoed from distant but unseen cliffs. Dragons and heroes fought endlessly against the coruscating backdrop of the aurora borealis, until the face of a very old woman, pale and haggard, appeared suddenly before him. "What more would you know?" she asked with fierce urgency, and then was gone. He fell again through the endless void. A word – 'Ginnungagap' – kept running through his head; it sounded familiar, but he could not remember where he had heard it before.

Snorri opened his eyes and wondered how long he had been asleep. He felt very refreshed, but completely disoriented. Had he slept through the night until dawn, or only until dusk? It had to be one or the other, to judge from the prevailing half-light. Who had put these rich, purple covers on his bed? Or was this his bed? If not, on whose bed was he lying? He became aware of a tall, shadowy figure standing next to him, felt rather than seen, just outside the range of vision.
"Where am I?" Snorri croaked.
"In Hel", came the whispered answer.
Snorri wondered why he was not upset, how he could take this terrible news so calmly. It simply didn't make sense to him. If he was in Hell, where were the flames? Where were the fiendish,

punishing demons? He inclined his head a little to the right, trying to get a better look at his neighbour.

"I didn't have time to make a confession..." he tried to explain. "The King sent them, the men with swords. I begged them not to strike, to give me time, but they slew me anyway. I have always been a good Christian and the priests said that..."

Sardonic laughter, a deep chuckle, cut short his protestations.

"This is not the fiery Hell of those priests", came the voice.

"Admittedly, some go to that place when they slough off their body-shirt, but their Christian faith is greater than yours, and they build that place of punishment for themselves even while they live. They make their choice. You, on the other hand, made yours. You spent much of your life remembering the old ways and reminding others of them. This is not the Hell of the White Christ; it is the Hel of your deepest memory and belief. Look around."

Anticipating some degree of effort (for he had no longer been young), Snorri found to his surprise that he simply drifted into a bolt-upright position. He was in some kind of hall, impressive in its vastness. There were no windows, nor were there any rush-torches or candles; despite that, the space was lit by a soft, sepia light. All around him in the dimly lit chamber were sleeping figures, resting on benches. Some seemed quite solid, others somehow mistier. A few were so vague that it was hard to make them out at all, except for tiny lights, like stars, that flickered where their head would have been. As he watched, one of these shapes vanished altogether. The star alone remained and it rose, drifted purposefully towards an open door, and was gone.

Snorri remained staring at the doorway for a long time, so many questions crowding upon him that he could no longer formulate them. Eventually he managed to gasp: "Who are all these... people? What is happening to them?"

The voice, hitherto mocking, replied in a comforting tone, as if from an elder brother. It seemed sad and at the same time uplifted, as if trying to convey a paradoxical truth.

"They are the dead... as you are, Snorri. They sleep and still dream... a little... but they will never wake again in the same form. Even now, they are being dismantled. Like you, they left their *lich*, their body-shirt, behind in Midgard. There they are being consumed by the worm and the mildew, and so give food to new growth. Much the same is happening to the final remnant of their other bodies, down here in Hel."

"Their other bodies?"

"The other parts that make up who a person is: the shade-body in which you sometimes travelled when asleep; thought and memory; self-awareness and self-delusion; the face you present to others... everything that makes a man more than a rock or a wooden log. All these are stripped away after death until only the soul remains, the tiny star that you perceived just now."

Snorri was aware of several more stars drifting out of the hall, even as they spoke. More questions formed themselves in his mind, but the acute wit and skill with words which had been his main assets in life seemed to be deserting him, and he found it difficult to express himself. His companion interrupted his musings.

"Come, Snorri. We must hurry, or you too may fade. It is a credit to the fact that you made yourself so solid, so self-aware, when you were alive that much of your being has made it intact down to Hel. Most humans are so insubstantial that they blow away after death, like chaff on the wind. In your case, only your physical body has gone."

Without effort, Snorri rose from the bed and stood before the visitor. This was actually quite pleasant, he reflected; all the old stiffness, all the aches and pains were gone now. If only he didn't feel that vague queasy, light-headed sensation as if bits of him wanted to go in different directions. The visitor seemed to read his thoughts and produced a golden torc, inscribed with mysterious symbols. He placed it around Snorri's neck and bent it so that it would stay on securely.

"Here, this will help you to hold together for as long as this takes, and protect you on the journey. Now mount the horse."

The horse, which Snorri had not perceived before and yet somehow had always been there, was huge, powerful and perfect. It was neither grey, nor roan, nor chestnut, nor black, and yet was all of these at the same time. It was pure equine essence, stomping with impatience to be away. His mysterious companion was already in the saddle.

"This is my steed, Galdrafaxi – Magic-mane - and to me the best of horses", he said and, reaching down, assisted Snorri to leap up behind him. Another doorway had appeared, and the horse and its riders shot through it like an arrow from a bow, outward and then upward. Snorri craned over his companion's shoulder to see that they were climbing almost vertically along a broad column of light. It was a busy road, it seemed, for they overtook many of the small, glowing stars that he had seen before. From the opposite direction came many shades of people, heading down to Hel. To his surprise, he seemed to recognise some of the latter.

"What may I call you?", he shouted to his guide against the rush of passing wind. Turning his head a little, the guide shouted back.

"I have many names, but you may call me Shiner."

# Chapter 2 - Svartálfheim

Soon they approached a land that reminded Snorri of the image of the Christian Hell, as preached to him ever since he had been a child, and he grew afraid. It was a dark land of rugged mountains, caverns and caves, illuminated mainly by the orange glow from many spewing flames and sparks. Over the land hung clouds of smoke, rolling, spiralling and lit from below by the fires. Against that sky, crenelated battlements, steeply pitched roofs and tall chimneys were starkly silhouetted. The effect of this daunting vision was augmented by the tumultuous noise issuing from within: deep, reverberating impacts that came at measured intervals, and mighty exhalations. As Galdrafaxi came to a halt, Snorri slid from the horse's back and felt the ground shake beneath his feet as he alighted. Looking tremulously up at his still-mounted companion, he asked "Dear God, have you brought me to Hell after all?" Shiner turned to glare at him for long seconds before uttering his rebuke. "No! As I have told you before, that place no longer holds any importance for you. Now, watch, listen and concentrate. My master has told me that you are a writer, and that much of what you wrote in life was wrong. It is his wish that you have an opportunity to learn, and my task is to provide that opportunity. In truth, it is something of an inconvenience to me, so do me a favour and be a quick learner."
A host of questions stormed into Snorri's mind but he fought them back, forcing himself instead to focus on his surroundings. They stood before a towering cliff, in which was set a colossal gate of wood and iron. As he watched, Shiner brought forth a wooden wand and traced patterns in the air, simultaneously uttering resonant and barbaric words. The patterns immediately reproduced themselves in glowing silver lines on the gate, giving rise to a crashing of opening locks and a thunderous rumble as the gate opened inward. At Shiner's bidding, Snorri mounted again and the steed carried them forward at a stately walk.

In the broad, cobbled courtyard where they now found themselves, they were met by a squat, powerful figure clad in armour and bearing axe and shield.

"Hail, Shiner!" came the greeting. "Welcome to Dark-Elf-Home. Thorin, son of Fundinn, greets you. Is this the burden of which we were warned?"

"A burden, aye, but a light one", Shiner replied with a laugh, "for this is the easiest part of my mission. Nevertheless, it is an important one and he must be brought before your Lord with all haste."

"Then I am at your service, Far-traveller", said the Dwarf with a slight bow, and took the reins of the horse.

Dismounting, Shiner led Snorri along a flagged pathway that wound ever upwards through canyons of granite and basalt. Snorri noticed that the walls of the canyons were carved in many places with elaborate friezes depicting, he assumed, great deeds and personages from the past. There was also Rune-script, but in a language unfamiliar to him. Eventually, a narrow passageway debouched into a broad place, brightly illuminated by scores of rush torches. Looking up, Snorri saw that the illumination was necessary because a huge, over-arching roof cut out the ambient light from the boiling, orange clouds. The roof was supported by many pillars of inestimable height. They were in a palace of cyclopean proportions. Two guards stood at the entrance to this palace, but had made no challenge. Clearly, they were expected.

There was something about the dimensions of the place that one part of Snorri's mind found disturbing and profoundly disorienting. It was all so vast – almost infinitely so – and yet intimate at the same time. An ornate fountain came into view, perhaps three hundred paces away, yet within a few steps they were already passing it. At first sight it had merely conveyed the essence of a fountain – extremely beautiful though the concept was – and then it acquired form and detail with each step that brought them closer. He noticed then that the same applied to all of the scene around him; nothing became detailed until he focused upon it. Another part of his mind begged him to relax and enjoy, and he followed this part, accepting and revelling in the strangeness without further question until it seemed the norm, as if things had ever been thus. Just a few paces further on (or had it been many miles?), Snorri felt a tug at the hem of his cloak and came to a halt. His attention had been drawn by his companion, who urgently whispered "You must focus now, Snorri. I know how difficult it is, until one acquires the art of such things. Look! We stand before the King of the Dwarfs. You would do well to kneel!"

Mind still in a pleasant haze, Snorri knelt as bidden and the act of kneeling seemed somehow symbolic on a deep level that he could not, as yet, identify. He had once knelt before a King - what was his name again? - but that had been out of custom and protocol. This was different, as if his action were a statement of a profound reality. Staring at the flagstones with bowed head as he chased the thought, he was pounded out of his reverie by the bass tones of a voice.

"Welcome, Snorri, son of Sturla! It is our pleasure to greet you in our hall. Come, rise and drink with us."

Snorri glanced for reassurance at Shiner, who also knelt at his side, and Shiner nodded approvingly. Snorri stood (again, the action seemed to take on some preternatural significance) and regarded his host, whom he perceived to be a Dwarf, but like no Dwarf he had ever conceived of in the mythology so laboriously penned in his living years. In the same way that the hall's dimensions had baffled and bewildered, the Dwarf King's size and appearance proved confusing to the mind. His host had, at one and the same time, what Snorri took to be a normal Dwarfish stature – about four and a half feet in height – and was yet immense. How could it be, that a being shorter than he could nevertheless tower over him? Other impressions of his eyes also contradicted the inner vision of his mind. As he raised his eyes from the flagstones before his feet, he took in a picture of stoutly-booted feet, strong short legs clad in leather breeches, a shirt of silver mail, powerful shoulders and neck and, finally, a swarthy, smiling face framed by flowing locks of brown hair. These prosaic observations were countered by different and somehow more real intimations that penetrated to his inner core: strength, solidity, stalwartness, power, cunning and, above all, wisdom.

As he held the benign gaze of the King of the Dwarfs, Snorri's attention was distracted by a servant bringing a horn of mead. He gladly took the horn and, raising it, said, in almost a whisper, "Wassail!" The King, smiling again, took the horn from his hands and signed and intoned runes over it. Then he passed it back with the words "Drink hail, friend Snorri; ever you sought wisdom, and wisdom shall be our gift."

Snorri drank deeply of the mead, in the correct way for such occasions, of three separate draughts – one for Odroerir, one for Son, and one for Bodn – in the manner that had always been passed on from father to son, despite the interference of the priests. It was coming back to him now. He passed the horn back to the servant who had brought it, and she held it out to Shiner. He took it with a nod and held it aloft. "Wassail, great King! We thank you for receiving us and for imparting your wisdom." Then he, too, drank three draughts and passed the horn to the servant, who returned it to the King.

The King sighed and, still holding the horn, ascended the three steps to his throne and sat down. "My name, as you should know, Snorri, is Móðsognir. I am the first and most ancient of all the Dwarf-kind. We do not impart our wisdom lightly to mortals, but I am commanded by the highest authority to make an exception in your case. It would appear that you made a great impression in your most recent spell in the Middle Garth. I am to instruct you concerning the nature and tasks of the Dwarfs, whom you also know as Dark Elves."

The mead's effect was pervading Snorri's entire system by now. Though a myriad of questions – mainly concerning the names and lineage of prominent Dwarfs – rose and fell in his mind, part of him immediately deemed them irrelevant. That part of him stood somewhere behind his mind, silent and watching. It could actually see the thoughts as small, brightly coloured lights, forming and emerging, drifting and coalescing, but ultimately always

disintegrating and vanishing. "Peace," said the Watcher, "be still and listen."
Móðsognir and Shiner smiled knowingly at each other as they saw the tranquillity descend on Snorri. Shiner chuckled and quoted:

"Let a man not be boastful about his wisdom,
but watchful instead. The wise and silent
are seldom harmed when wary in the hall.
A more trustworthy friend,
a man cannot have,
than understanding."

"Indeed", replied the King, and continued. "Snorri, the draught has prepared you to accept wisdom. Now you must forget all you knew, and keep your eyes and ears open. Follow me."

With that, the King rose nimbly from his throne and, within a few paces, was already leaving the hall. Snorri and Shiner hastened after him as he strode along an enclosed pathway in the direction of the roaring, hammering noise Snorri had perceived earlier. The pathway was open from above, and an orange light shone on the walls to either side. These walls were covered in friezes that shifted, flowed and solidified again under his gaze. There seemed to be no permanence here unless he stared fixedly at something; everything was either coming into existence or fading from it. Leaving the pathway, they encountered a scene that would have overwhelmed Snorri's senses but for the calming effect of the mead he had drunk. All across a vast plain there were buildings of every shape, size and age, some apparently new while others crumbled and sank into the muddy ground that surrounded them. All were lit only by the flickering flames of innumerable fires, and the sky above would have been dark but for the glow cast on rising, drifting clouds of smoke and vapour. This bewildering landscape was populated by hundreds of busy figures, constantly labouring at forges and foundries, hauling carts of materials to and fro, or loading and unloading them. In addition to the host of impressions that his eyes were forced to take in, Snorri's ears were assaulted by a barrage of sound from pounding hammers, rumbling wheels and the exhalations of many bellows. The King looked back over his shoulder, beckoned for them to hurry, and with Shiner's comforting presence still at his side, Snorri hastened to follow. They arrived at a line of rail trucks, and he finally saw what their cargo was; it consisted of dead humans. Dwarfs were hauling the corpses from the trucks and disassembling them, taking the flesh from the bones, starting with the softer parts such as the eyes and tongue and continuing until nought remained but the skeleton. Then even the bones were ground to dust, though a few were taken and passed along the line for some other purpose. Gazing at the Dwarfs as they went cheerfully about their work, Snorri had a sudden image of worms, centipedes and fungi; it came as a flash and was gone again, like a picture momentarily glimpsed when flicking rapidly through the pages of a book. It occurred to him that he ought to find it all horrifying, or at the very least distasteful, but it did not feel like that at all. Instead, he found it quite natural and extremely fascinating. He became aware that the King was speaking again.

"Aye, this is part of the dismantling process. Everything contained in this dead material is taken apart and will be used again. It's all useful stuff! You'll have eaten a lot of it, indirectly, during your time on Midgard."

Snorri paused for a moment, puzzled.

"I have eaten dead humans? How can that be? It is a sin, and I would never willingly do so!"

The King rolled his eyes and addressed himself first to Shiner.

"I thought you said you had brought me one of the clever ones? He doesn't seem too bright. Look, Snorri", he continued, "Did you ever hear the expression 'pushing up daisies' for someone who is dead? What do you think feeds those daisies? Or the grass that feeds your sheep and kine? So - *indirectly* - have you not eaten the dead?"

Snorri looked down, shamefaced, and resolved to think henceforth before opening his mouth.

"All good stuff", boomed the King, warming to his subject, "but there's one bit that's very difficult to recycle... and that's the

arsehole! So we send a lot of those straight back up to be people again without further ado. Isn't that so, lads?!"
A roar of laughter came from the working Dwarfs. One of them chimed in "Yes, and they say the biggest arseholes get to be kings and queens!", then realised too late whose company he was in. With a casual swipe of his powerful arm, the King knocked him in a parabolic arc over the trucks and into the distance, the Dwarf's receding shriek ending abruptly as he landed with a shower of sparks in a furnace. The King sniffed and shrugged.
"Now back to work, the lot of you! Come on, Snorri, come on Mister Shiner, we have much yet to see and no time to waste."

He led them up the line, instructing as he walked, clearly enjoying this rare opportunity to be a tour guide.
"Now those lads you just saw, they're a good lot and they perform an essential function, but when it comes down to it they are what you might call unskilled labour, and not the sharpest axes in the hoard. You'll find the real craftsmen in the next department, although strictly speaking it's the first department."
Together they strode on until they stood by the doorway of a workshop. Unlike the previous venue, it was roofed and completely enclosed. The closed door was adjacent to a portal through which trucks passed along the railway; one of these exited from the workshop as they stood, brushing aside hanging strips of leather. The King lowered his voice.
"We'll have to be quiet in here, and if you have any questions then keep your voice down. The work is of a very delicate and difficult nature, and my workers need to concentrate."
He quietly opened the door and ushered them in. It was much quieter in here, being to some extent insulated from the impacts and exhalations that prevailed outside. There was also plentiful lighting where needed, though Snorri noticed that some of the Dwarfs preferred to work in shadow and wore blinkers on each side of their face to cut out extraneous light. All of these Dwarfs, he saw, were of the older and more thoughtful type - serious, and clearly devoted to their work. The King sought out one of them and

beckoned him over. The Dwarf bowed to the King, then examined Snorri with gimlet eyes as the King spoke.

"Hail, Master Glóin. I have a task for you. I would like you to instruct this unusual human, Snorri Sturluson, concerning the nature of your work. There is no need to disturb your craftsmen, but do let him know exactly what you do here, and why."

The foreman nodded his assent, then beckoned Snorri to follow him. Shiner remained with the King by the door.

"This way, Sir", said Glóin, "might as well take you to the top of the shop, where they come in. That way you'll see the process from the start and it will all make more sense."

They made their way past the row of workbenches. Though Snorri could not see over the shoulders of the quietly toiling artisans, he saw the occasional glow or flicker of light in various colours, and once heard an uttered "Drat!" as someone laboured with a particularly fiddly task. Eventually they reached the far side of the workshop where the trucks entered, again through a portal hung with strips of leather. A truck rolled in, and it contained a corpse, neatly clothed and respectfully arrayed with arms crossed over the chest. The lips were moving and the eyes were open.

"That one's not dead", Snorri exclaimed, though to his surprise it came out as a simple statement of perceived fact rather than a cry of horror. The Watcher at the back of his mind reminded him that the enchanted mead was still having its effect.

"You are wrong, Sir", replied the foreman, "quite dead. She just don't know it yet. Common occurrence." He gave the woman's shoulder a comforting pat.

"Don't you worry, my dear. We'll soon have you sorted out."

The foreman turned back to Snorri as the truck and its content rolled quietly along the greased rail to the first workbench and attendant Dwarf.

"You see, Sir, sometimes they comes in quiet as lambs having made their peace up there. Them's the ones that knows they're dead, having expected it all along, like. Then they're just like sleeping babes, and easiest to work with. Others are a bit confused. The worst ones is them what the Valkyries missed by some oversight:

just died in battle an' still thinks they're fighting. Can't do us no harm, of course, but they got a right *hamr* on them and we have to calm 'em down before we can get busy. Worst one I can remember, it was some berserker, we had to use some of that chain left over from the binding of Fenrir. Quite a day that was." He chuckled.
"Anyway, let's have a look at what Fili here is doing. He's our apprentice, so he gets to deal with them as they first come in and do the least delicate work. He also gets to deal with the raging ones, but it's all good experience and he can call on me for assistance if he needs it."
The foreman moved to stand behind Fili, a mere youth of a Dwarf whose beard was only seven inches long.
"Everything alright, Fili?"
"Yes, Mister Foreman. All routine stuff, this one."
The woman in front of Fili continued to speak, though only a skilled lip-reader could make out her words, for she had no breath. In truth, it came down to reading thoughts, for she still had those, and Snorri found that they came across as clearly as if they had been spoken.
"Remember to water the plants. Don't spend the money all at once. Sorry I have to leave you. Am I dead now?"
Fili looked at the dead woman intently, and Snorri saw a single tear course down the Dwarf's cheek and into his beard. Fili took up something that looked like a long pair of tweezers, gulped, and spoke to the dead woman.
"You are dead now, and you can rest. I'm just going to sort out your cognition, then you can sleep." More tears ran down Fili's face. He reached inside the head with the tweezers, meeting no physical opposition, then probed briefly, brought out something angular, and dropped it into a kidney-shaped tray with a small clang. He rested his head on his chest and breathed deeply as the woman's speech ceased and her eyes closed.
Foreman Glóin patted the boy's shoulder approvingly.
"Nice one, Fili. Take a minute if you want. Empathy shows you are a good Dwarf, but you'll learn not to let it rule you."

The truck silently moved one place further, and Snorri and Glóin quietly stepped behind the next craftsman, an older Dwarf whose head was bald but whose beard hung to his waist. In hushed tones, Glóin explained what was happening.

"The first bit, removing the capacity for thought, is the easiest part. That's why we start our apprentices on that task. The next, removing the memories, is a lot trickier, so we give it to one of our most experienced operatives. Fundinn is a dab hand at it; even I can learn one or two things from him."

Snorri watched as the Dwarf went about his task with a collection of strange, delicate instruments. From the woman's crown he enticed a tangled skein of glowing threads and, after some searching, located a free end. Using a small dab of glue to secure the end, he carefully began to wind the thread onto a glass rod, turning it by means of a crank. Snorri saw that the Dwarf had a small, tubular device jammed into his right eye socket; apparently it helped him to see better. As if he had read Snorri's mind, Fundinn removed the device, looked back over his shoulder and offered it to Snorri. With some help from the foreman, Snorri placed the tube over his own right eye and examined the thread closely. The tube made everything appear bigger, and now he could see that the thread was made up of tiny, moving images. Here was a smiling, female face and a hand holding out a spoonful of porridge; then a garden in springtime, the air filled with dandelion seeds. A familiar lullaby came unbidden to his ears, and he realised he was watching the woman's earliest memories. At the realisation, he felt a little embarrassed; it felt like voyeurism, so he removed the device from his eye and handed it back to Fundinn with muttered thanks. The Dwarf smiled, nodded and returned to his work. The memories consisted of numerous separate threads, crossing each other and sometimes branching and diverging, as if the owner had held different memories of the same event. The hues varied. Some glowed with a bright, golden light, while others were dull and ugly, like the colour of a bruise. Meticulously, Fundinn teased the threads apart, categorised them, and rolled them onto separate rods. The rods were then slid into tubes of some clear material Snorri could not identify, and carefully labelled. An urgent question arose in Snorri's mind.

"What happens to the memories? Where do our memories go after we are dead?"

He noticed Fundinn stiffen slightly and stop winding, though he did not look up. Glóin shuffled his feet slightly, cleared his throat and appeared to think carefully about his next words.

"Mister Snorri, Sir… if you are anything like as important as what rumour would have it, I expect you will be told in due course. All I can tell you is that the Boss wants 'em, and I expect he has his reasons."

"The Boss?", Snorri replied. "You mean your King, Móðsognir?"

A sudden hush fell across the entire row of benches, and Snorri could sense all the Dwarfs in the workshop listening while pretending to be working. Glóin´s eyes flicked over his small but essential fiefdom, then he pulled back his shoulders and looked straight at Snorri with a deadpan expression.

"No Sir, I do not mean our revered King, important though he is. It is my understanding that you are here on the orders of a higher authority, and I cannot tell you more than that, if you do not already know it yourself."

He looked around the workshop and spoke in a quiet but commanding voice.

"Eyes on your jobs, lads!", and the Dwarfs devoted their full attention to their work again.

They passed down the line, observing each of the craftsmen as he removed some essential part of a dead person's being: the emotions, the skills, the experience, and the persona. The Dwarf in charge of removing the latter prised gently at a point on the edge of the face. There was a click, and a ghostly mask came away in his hands. The corpse still had a face, but now it was bland, expressionless and devoid of character. The mask, like all the other parts, was carefully packed and stored for some future use. At the last bench, several Dwarfs worked together, apparently stroking and pulling at the body, but with their hands a few inches above its

surface, until something came loose and drifted free of it. To his astonishment, Snorri saw that it was an exact replica of the dead person, but thin, etheric and insubstantial. Behind the point where the eyes would have been, a bright, white light shone like a star. He was reminded of the host of drifting stars that he had observed in that quiet hall, where he had awoken after his own violent end.
"Is that the person's shade?", he asked.
"Well done, you're learning", the foreman replied, "but we call it the *hamr*. It's with you all your life, but most people are barely aware of it. When you're healthy and vibrant, it can extend some way beyond what you call your body. Ever had somebody move close to you, perhaps unseen, and felt uncomfortable? That's because their hamr had invaded your hamr's space. Some people can get the hamr to leave the hard body while it sleeps, and ride on it to go wherever they like. Or they can change its shape, and give themselves a different appearance. Now it's the last part of this person that we are really interested in. It is the ship that will carry that little white light, the soul, onward to its resting place in Hel. The rest is just meat, and you've already seen the dismantling process for that."
The Dwarfs gently, respectfully, helped the hamr to stand upright, then guided it towards a separate exit that Snorri had not previously noticed. It drifted rather than walked, moving without protest through the doorway, and was gone. He turned and saw that the foreman was examining him minutely and with great interest.
"With your permission, Mister Snorri?" Glóin passed his hands over Snorri's head and shoulders, stroked his arm down to the elbow, then took both his hands and examined them carefully. Still holding his hands, he searched Snorri's face with critical, slightly narrowed eyes.
"So what am I looking at here?", he muttered. "All your thoughts and memory still intact. Persona still in place. Hamr nearly as solid as I am. You're a rare one, and no mistake. How did you get past my department? Can't have been an accident... we don't make that kind of mistake. Sometimes a hamr gets away unguarded, if we

don't take out all the memories properly, and makes a nuisance of itself up there in Midgard; but you… you're different."
He stopped speaking and looked up and behind Snorri. "You keep that torc on your neck, Mister Snorri. Don't you go flying apart."
Then, suddenly, Shiner and the King were back. The King clapped an arm around Snorri's shoulders in avuncular fashion. He was clearly having fun, but still kept his voice low.
"Thank you, Master Glóin, for an excellent exposition of your art!" The foreman bowed.
"Snorri, I hope that you have learned much", the King continued. "Now it is time to show you the constructive side of our work."
All the Dwarfs in the workshop rose, bowed towards the King and Snorri, then returned silently to their labours.

They were already back on the cinder path that wove between the various workshops and smithies, Snorri jogging to keep up with the striding King of the Dwarfs. Shiner pulled a flask from within his cloak and passed it to Snorri.
"Here, take another draught", he hissed. "It's the same mead that you drank before. Drink some more so that you can keep up and absorb all you see without being overwhelmed."
Snorri drank deeply, and immediately felt the benefit. Once again, he felt as though he had three-league boots on, and the scenes he had recently witnessed seemed less disquieting. Stepping out easily behind the King, he took in all the individual scenes that they passed. Under a flame-lit sky of shifting smoke, he saw sturdy Dwarfs hard at work everywhere. The clangour of hammers and the roar of bellows formed a constant background din that almost overpowered his senses. The ground vibrated beneath his feet, and the air was heavy with the acrid odours of soot and hot metal. To Snorri's right, Dwarf smiths forged swords and spears in a manner that was thoroughly familiar to him, but to his left they were making strange tubes of iron. In an adjacent workshop, these tubes were being fitted with oddly-shaped wooden handles and intricate mechanisms. Further on, other Dwarfs were building massive carts that were made entirely of metal and had wheels without spokes.

Passing yet another workshop, there was a click followed by a flash, and Snorri was stunned by a loud report that momentarily deafened him, and the accompanying gout of flame blinded him.

"Hey, careful where you point that thing!", bellowed the Dwarf King, and struck the offending Dwarf a swinging clap. The King turned to look at Snorri, assessing whether any real harm had been done.

"Ha!", he exclaimed, seeing that Snorri was only shocked. "That will have pulled your threads back together pretty well! You won't be needing any of that special mead for a while." And he laughed; a deep, rumbling chuckle.

"Wh… what was that thing?", Snorri stammered.

"A weapon", the King replied, "a weapon of war, and for the hunt, but not of your time. We make things here for the men of every age, some of them deadly like that tube, but most of them we make for more constructive purposes. Now let us move on, for I am proud of my realm and there is much to show you in the short time you can be with us."

For the next hour – or was it a year? Snorri could not say which – he was treated to a display of Dwarven manufacturing until they finally stepped out into a place that seemed somewhat brighter, as if day were dawning. Indeed, a pleasant chorus of birdsong was clearly audible. Out of the corner of his eye, he thought he saw the sun rise, but when he turned his head he saw that he must have been mistaken, for it had not yet risen. Before him stood a long line of what looked like people, though he could only see their backs. They were naked, slightly transparent, and appeared not quite solid, though they were rapidly acquiring solidity as they approached the head of the long queue. A couple of elder Dwarfs consulted a list, written in runes, and directed other Dwarfs about their work. The Dwarfish artisans were fitting masks to the passive, human-like figures. Occasionally, when a mask proved a poor fit, it was taken back and exchanged for another one, or the mask had small adjustments made to it between anvil and tapping hammer, and then the fit was tried again. Right at the head of the queue, Snorri was bidden to stop and focus on the procedure. Standing between

Shiner and the King, he watched as a Dwarf retrieved one of the now-familiar small lights from a glass jar. Using long tweezers, the Dwarf inserted the light into the head of a patient, immobile figure. The eyes instantly opened. Now another Dwarf approached the figure, carrying in his hand an inscribed parchment. Placing his mouth close to the figure's ear, he began "This is your Wyrd…" Snorri could not hear the rest. As the recital ended, the figure nodded, walked away towards the rising sun, and was lost to view against the light.

Snorri gasped, and the King patted him on the shoulder.

"Well, that's it, boy", he said. "We showed you how we take 'em apart, and now we've shown how we make 'em anew, and many other things besides. Time for you to get going again. Shiner, what has he seen so far?"

"Only Hel and your realm, Your Majesty."

"Only two?!", the King exclaimed. "Then you had better hurry if you are to see all of it before you unravel completely. If I'd known, I would not have detained you so long. Now, be off with you!"

Snorri and Shiner both bowed and thanked the King. Shiner's marvellous steed had suddenly and mysteriously reappeared, and they mounted it, Snorri again sitting behind Shiner. At the latter's bidding, Galdrafaxi galloped skyward along a broad road of pure light. The air rushed about them, greenish and scintillating like the Northern Lights so commonly seen in Snorri's native Iceland. He leaned forward and shouted to Shiner.

"Where are we going now? What realm am I now to visit?"

"We are riding to the realm of the Wanes, whom you know as Vanir", he replied. "They are mighty Gods, though you wrote but little about them while you were alive."

Snorri felt somewhat goaded by the criticism.

"I wrote as much as was preserved in our lore", he responded defensively. "No record remained of their land, only the doings of those who lived among the Aesir… and of those precious little."

Shiner smiled, and Snorri wondered how he could know that Shiner was smiling, even though his face was turned away and hidden by a hood.

"Then you may be starting to understand how privileged you are to make this journey", said Shiner. "Be glad that you have been marked out as a special case."

# Chapter 3 - Vanaheim

Thus rebuked, Snorri sat back and took in his surroundings. The phosphorescent air seemed to become even brighter and distinctly warmer. Previously, it had been chilly, even freezing, as on a high mountain top, but now it was as pleasant as a mild day in spring. He looked ahead again, and saw that they were rapidly approaching a portal from which a dazzling green-and-gold light issued. The circle of light grew ever wider as they sped toward it, and in an instant they had arrived. Shiner swung his left leg over the horse's mane and dismounted; Snorri followed suit and slid to the ground. He felt springy turf under his feet and perceived that they were standing in a broad, sunlit meadow. At least, he could make out colours and the vague forms of bushes and flowers, but though the colours were of a brilliance that seemed unimaginable, everything else appeared blurred and indistinct as though he were seeing it through water. Birdsong filled the air, far more melodious than anything he had hitherto experienced, and the delicious fragrance of blossom met his nostrils. Snorri blinked hard several times and rubbed at his eyes, but the landscape refused to come into focus. He could vaguely make out Shiner standing before him, and Shiner's garb had also acquired a brilliant hue that he had not noticed before. Someone else stood next to Shiner, a being of light and shifting colours who seemed to inhale and exhale the delightful but formless surroundings. The being handed something to Shiner, and Shiner said to Snorri "Here, let me put this on you. It will help you to see." Carefully he fitted the object to Snorri's face, and everything was brought into sharp focus. Snorri's fingers explored the artefact: two pieces of round glass, held within frames; an arch that sat upon the bridge of his nose, and long projections on each side that sat on the tops of his ears. He removed them briefly, and all was blurry again; replacing them, all came once more into focus. He looked the welcomer up and down, and what he saw was an apparition of beauty. Light radiated from the handsome face, shining from within. The hair that crowned the head was as fine as thistle-down,

but golden. The being was tall and slender, and his – or was it her? – clothes changed and shifted in iridescent waves of colour.
Snorri fell to his knees, mouth agape.
"Are… are you an angel?", he managed to gasp.
The welcomer looked puzzled and turned to Shiner for an explanation. Shiner, however, had lost his customary composure and was having a fit of laughter. Eventually, taking a deep and deliberate breath, he calmed himself and said to their host "*Hann er kristinn* – he's a Christian, and he thinks you are a messenger sent from his god." Turning to Snorri, he continued.
"Snorri, I told you already to put all that nonsense out of your head. If you want a god, then you are in the presence of one: this is a Wane!"
Snorri mumbled apologies, but Shiner was already hauling him to his feet. He spoke sternly.
"Come on, Snorri. Time is short, and there is much to see. We are going to meet the King of the Wanes. Be silent; best to speak when you are spoken to. Wear the perspective-glasses, and take another draught of this mead. But neither eat nor drink anything that is offered from now on, unless I give leave, otherwise you may wish to remain here forever, and that is not permitted."

The three set off, walking across the broad meadow towards a verdant forest with the horse Galdrafaxi trailing behind them. The crushing awe that had at first overwhelmed Snorri evaporated, and now he felt nought but joy. Elated, he soon ignored Shiner's order to be silent and sang a children's song about the coming of spring, and even skipped across the sward. Neither Shiner nor the welcomer seemed to mind, but instead shared smiling and indulgent glances. Soon they were at the fringe of the wood, negotiating a path that led between tall nettles and foxgloves, and before long a tall canopy of leaves and branches all but shut out the sunlight, enveloping them in a chlorophyl gloom. Unafraid, Snorri drank in all the sights, sounds and fragrances of the leafy twilight. Despite the lack of light, the colours still entranced him, the resplendent essence of abundant Nature. There were leaves of every shade of green, and flowers of yellow, purple and red. From the forest floor rose toadstools, brown and ghostly white, and the air was heavy with the musky scent of their spores. They continued along the woodland path until they came to a small cottage set in a clearing. The cottage was constructed from oaken beams inset with wattle-and-daub panels, and it was roofed with wooden shingles. Red roses encompassed the doorway, and it was surrounded on all sides by a neat garden containing vegetable plots and flower beds. At one of the plots, two people worked with trowels as they kneeled on rush mats.  They appeared quite old, their skins wrinkled and tanned, and they wore simple, peasant clothing and wide-brimmed, straw hats. Apart from the buzz of industrious bees among the flowers,  it was a scene of perfect tranquillity. Snorri discerned beehives behind the tall poles that supported a luxuriant growth of pea and bean plants.

Shiner pushed Snorri in the small of his back, propelling him towards the two old people. Snorri, puzzled, looked back over his shoulder and received a reassuring nod from Shiner, and another from their Vanic welcomer. He walked forward along the path that separated the flower beds, coming to a halt to the right of the old man. The latter, seeing Snorri's shadow, simply said "Hello, young man. Would you mind passing me the fork from that basket over there?" Snorri looked about him, saw a wicker basket filled with gardening tools, selected a short-handled fork and passed it to the man, who thanked him and carried on working. The man and woman had trays of seedlings and were planting them into black, fertile loam. Occasionally, the two would comment something to each other, make a joke, or pass a criticism. The criticisms were met with an accustomed humour, and Snorri sensed the love that passed between them. Their occupation fascinated him. In life, he had never had much time or taste for gardening, and had spent most of his time writing poetry, travelling, and attending the courts of kings, but he remembered how his foster-grandmother had planted beds of flowers on the home acre, right next to the turf cottage where he had grown up. His grandfather had grumbled at

the waste of grazing space, but she had persisted and created a little beauty in that otherwise harsh and utilitarian landscape. Assailed by a compelling whim, he spoke to the gardeners.
"Please may I help you?", he asked.
They both looked up at him with eyes that reflected the blue sky and the green of the woods, and then they looked to each other in a second of silent consultation.
"Yes, of course, young man", said the woman, "but you had better wear this hat. The sun is very strong today. Here, let me find you a trowel and a fork, and a mat to kneel on."
Snorri was allotted a tray of seedlings to plant, and for the rest of the afternoon he devoted his time to what seemed the most joyful and worthwhile labour that he had ever undertaken. Sometimes he made a mistake, and either the old man or the old woman would gently correct him. The shoots that he planted grew at a prodigious rate, and curious bees hovered ever before him, as if trying to make out what business he had to be there.

At the end of the afternoon, as the sun was sinking towards the horizon and appearing only in random rays through the trees, the old peasants straightened up and surveyed their work. Snorri saw then that his tray of seedlings, and several more, were now empty, and the bed was completely planted. He stood, but his knees did not crack, nor were his shoulders stiff. On the contrary, he felt very good. His eyes straying to a plot of cabbage, he noticed something that he first took to be a very small mushroom, but it was moving. Taking a few paces toward it, he saw that it was a miniscule, human-looking creature; at least, it had two legs, two arms, a torso and a head, and it walked upright. Its skin was brown, it wore a pale, broad-brimmed hat, and it was pushing a tiny wheelbarrow full of leafy detritus. As it pushed, it muttered to itself. Snorri could not understand the words, but the tone suggested that it was cursing its labour. He turned around to ask the old man and woman about it, but they had gone. The sun had set and the bluish shade of dusk had settled on the garden, so he walked to the cottage, whose windows now emitted a welcoming, yellow light. A gentle downpour of rain had begun. He knocked at the door and entered to find Shiner and the guide sitting on a bench at a table, chatting amiably, holding drinking horns and apparently in good spirits. They looked around as Snorri entered.

"Hey, Snorri!", called Shiner in a slightly slurred voice. "We have been waiting all afternoon for you. Did you have fun? Come and join us!"

"Might I first wash my hands?", Snorri replied. "They must be very…" He was going to say 'dirty' but looking at his hands, he saw to his surprise that they were perfectly clean and smooth. He had expected to see grime in every wrinkle, dirty finger nails, and even a blister or two on the palms, but they were immaculate. Nor was there any trace of soil on the knees of his trousers. Before he could get over his astonishment, Shiner bade him again to come and sit. Without any conscious movement, he found himself seated at the table. A horn appeared in his hand, though he could not recall anyone having brought it to him.

"Good health!" said Shiner, and tapped Snorri's horn with his own. Snorri started to raise the horn, then lowered it.

"Wait a minute, Shiner", he said, "you told me that I must neither drink nor eat here without your leave. What is this?"

Shiner's sparkling eyes (he had not really noticed those eyes before) bored for an instant deep into his own, evincing deep admiration. "Well done, Snorri!", he said in a low voice, still holding Snorri's gaze. "You are clearly not the foolish human that I first took you for. Before you could have taken sip, I would have dashed the horn from your hand, but you have passed the test."

With that, he traced a sign over the horn and continued "Now you can drink. It is safe."

Reassured, Snorri raised the horn to his lips, took a sip, and tasted wine more delicious and refreshing than any he had tasted at the courts of kings. He took a deeper draught, and surveyed the inside of the cottage. To his astonishment, it was considerably larger on the inside than it had appeared from the outside: a substantial hall, in fact. Above him was a wooden ceiling supported by pillars, richly carved with runes and foliate decoration. He tried to read the runes, but they were beyond his ken; unlike the angular Futhark, with which he was fairly well acquainted, these curved and flowed and resembled the patterns to be found on the bark and leaves of trees. The walls of the hall were hung with elaborate, finely woven and colourful tapestries, most of them with a pastoral or agricultural theme, but some with hunting scenes. The hall was lit with candles made not of tallow, but of beeswax. As they burned, they gave off a pleasant, herbal aroma. Snorri examined more closely one of those that lit the table, and saw that it was infused with small particles of ground herbs. In one corner of the hall was a staircase protected by a balustrade, and that impressed Snorri even more: it indicated that the cottage had another floor above the ceiling overhead. Such luxury was almost unknown in the world that he had inhabited in life. Down those stairs now came a man and a woman, and Snorri stood, for he could see from their fine dress that they must be royalty. They were both clad in garments that shimmered like silk, green and gold, and they wore golden circlets about their brows. Shiner and their guide also stood as a sign of respect, and bowed their heads.

"Hail, my Lord and Lady", said Shiner, and the handsome pair inclined their heads, smiling, in response.
"Welcome, Shiner", replied the man. "And this must be Snorri Sturluson, about whom we have heard so much?" Both the lord and the lady regarded Snorri with eyes that were as young as the dawn and as ancient as the stars. Under that penetrating gaze, Snorri almost forgot his manners, but then recovered himself and said "Snorri Sturluson, at your service, my Lord and Lady."
"Snorri", said Shiner, "this is Lord Algróinn of the Vanir, and his consort, the Lady Vanadís. Lord Algróinn is the son of Vanafaðir, King of the Vanir. Our guide, whom you have already met, is Vaxandi, their nephew." Vaxandi nodded and smiled.

Again, there was that dreamlike, unaccountable shift in circumstances, and Snorri found himself sitting again at the table, but facing the lord and lady and with Shiner on his right and Vaxandi on his left. He noticed that the table was now decked with all kinds of enticing food – meats, fish, green vegetables and freshly baked bread. His mouth watered, but he waited patiently until Shiner had cast a rune over all that was offered and indicated that Snorri might partake freely. Then Snorri ravenously ate his fill of all the flesh, fowl and fish, and of all the greens and the several types of fresh bread. So delicious was the food that he fancied his taste buds must have been benumbed during all his earthly existence. Of the wine, too, he partook freely; it loosened his word-hoard and encouraged him to pose the myriad questions that entered his mind. His hosts, who ate more sparsely and decorously, seemed not to mind his torrent of questions.

"It is so wonderful to be here!", Snorri blurted. "Here, in the realm of the Vanir, of all places! A realm of which I have heard less, perhaps, than all others. I can list all the heavenly homes of the Aesir, and even of the Vanir – Niord, Freyr and Freya – who dwell among the Aesir, but of the Vanir and their native homes I know next to nothing. You fought with the Aesir in the beginning, I heard, and you were winning! You forced them to exchange hostages! Please tell me more about that."

Algróinn took a sip of wine, sighed, and cast his eyes about the carven beams as though they might tell the tale of the episode, which indeed they did, had Snorri but been able to read the runes. "That was an unfortunate business", he said. "We are not warlike Gods, but we know how to wage war when we must. When we fight, we charge fiercely like the tusky boar, and with all the force of brute Nature. The Aesir, with all their knowledge and cunning, had not reckoned on such power. They counted on their science and their artefacts, their spears and axes, and their tactics, but we tripped them with roots and pounded them with floods. They were at our mercy, but it was never our intention to destroy them, so we accepted an armistice and exchanged hostages."

Snorri thought for a moment, rubbing a finger along the waxed surface of his drinking-horn, and asked "So how did the war start?" Algróinn pressed his eyelids together and grimaced, as if remembering in pain. "We were… indiscreet", he said.
"Undiplomatic. Realise that these were the primaeval days when we, too, had much to learn. We saw the manner in which the Aesir were proceeding about their business. It was all of iron, so hard and edged, and we sought to soften that. So we sent one of our own among them to teach them a different way, a way to make things softly, as the golden light of sunrise casts ephemeral diamonds on the grass. But they were not interested in her teachings. They lusted for the diamonds and the gold, and blamed her for making them desirous of gold. Gullveig – 'Gold-greedy' – they called her, and said she was a witch. They mistreated her, burned her and stabbed her. Still she lived, but we could not ignore the insult. And thus we went to war. All Yggdrasil quivered with the shock as our forces met!"
At the mention of Yggdrasil, Snorri pricked up his ears, for here was a mystery that had always intrigued him.
"You mention Yggdrasil, the World-Tree", he said. "I have always wished to know the origin of that great tree. Its name means the column, or pole, of Yggr – who is Odin – but nowhere in our lore is it mentioned how the tree came into being."
Algróinn laughed then. It was one of those deep, nearly silent laughs, the laughter of a person who is trying to conceal his merriment but failing. His chest heaved, his mouth was curved in a grin, and tears of mirth ran down his cheeks as he held his hand to his mouth and looked away. Vaxandi and Vanadís giggled too, and Shiner pursed his lips and earnestly pretended not to have heard the question. Snorri looked on, totally confused, until Algróinn could contain himself no longer and gave a great guffaw, which was joined with relief by all except for the bewildered Snorri. Finally, and apparently with a little embarrassment, Algróinn regained his composure, wiped his eyes, and drew a deep breath.
"Oooooh, but that was our biggest joke and accomplishment! Of course your lore tells nothing of it, for you humans are the

creatures of Odin, and he is hardly likely to tell you that others had a hand in the ordering of the nine worlds." He leaned towards Snorri, and his tone became confidential. Vanadís was impassive, but Snorri could tell from the glances between Shiner and Vaxandi that something tremendous was about to be imparted. Algróinn reached out, stroking the back of Snorri's right hand and focusing his gaze upon it. He seemed lost in thought, but then abruptly looked him in the eye and continued in a low voice "Mister Snorri, you are a strange one. I know little of you or of your worth, but the one you call Allfather has requested me, for the sake of the peace between our realms and races, to tell you all, and to tell it honestly. You must count a lot for him." He took a deep draught from his horn, and Vanadís smiled sympathetically and took his arm in her own as Shiner and Vaxandi breathlessly awaited the revealing of a mystery to the mere mortal.

"It was like this, you see", Algróinn went on. "You thought that Buri, Odin's grandfather, was the only unusual thing that emerged from the primaeval chaos after the Becoming, when giants ruled supreme. Buri begat a son, Borr – I don't know how, I wasn't around at the time, but presumably he mated with one of the Etin-kin – and Borr mated with another Etin-wife, Bestla, to produce three fine sons: Odin, Vili and Vé. Those sons grew up, and... you know the rest. Well, old Buri wasn't the only new thing lurking in that world of fog, frost and spitting fire. There was a little patch of moss that took hold among the ice. It didn't want much, just some water, a bit of heat, and whatever nutrients were around. Nobody noticed it, but it expanded and became conscious. From it was born Laufgróðr – Leaf-Growth – the father of all the Vanir. We multiplied and prospered, and we had a hand in shaping Midgard, for from us comes all organic growth: every leaf and blade of grass, every forest and every beast. We populated Midgard with these things, but we did something much more extraordinary than that. The multiverse that Odin and his brothers were creating would have been a structure of stone and iron but, unbeknown to them, we planted a seed that sprouted and grew into the tree you call Yggdrasil. Its roots and branches support all the Nine Worlds, and its existence came as a complete surprise to Odin! He had thought that he and his brethren were alone in reshaping everything after the slaying of Ymir, and was astonished to find that the overall structure had grown organically, and was not of his making. That was our jest, and our greatest achievement."

All this talk of growth led Snorri's thoughts back to the afternoon he had spent planting seedlings in the garden outside, and of the small creature he had seen in the dusk. He spoke of it now.
"I passed a most pleasant afternoon in the company of two old gardeners", he said. "I had never imagined that it could be so enjoyable and absorbing to tend plants but, just before I came in, I noticed a small being that I first took for a mushroom. However, it was walking and pushing a little wheelbarrow full of leaf mould. What was that thing?"
"That", replied Algróinn, "was an Etin."
Snorri's eyes opened wide in surprise. "An Etin? But it was so small! I thought Etins were huge, hulking beings. And why would there be Etins in this beautiful place of growth?"
Now it was Vaxandi who answered him. "They are here because we need them, and not all Etins are gigantic. Some are so small that you cannot see them at all. You speak of a beautiful place of growth, but unbridled growth is a curse and a failing – even here. Did you ever, in life, get a chance to watch peasants at work in the summer? Perhaps not so much in your native Iceland, but in more southerly climes. They constantly have to weed and hoe their standing crops, otherwise their acres would become choked and overgrown with weeds. The same applies here – especially here, the very home and heart of organic growth. There must be balance, and we cannot provide this ourselves. Everything we touch grows, but a tree that is not pruned eventually ceases to bear fruit. That is why we employ Etins. They prune, and they smite some of the growth with Death on a daily basis, and then they carry away the dead matter to compost-heaps to provide rich loam in which future growth can take root. They always complain about the work that we

put upon them, but that is in their nature. We do not mix with them or invite them to sup with us. You might say that it is a business arrangement, and they get their rewards."

Snorri was feeling rather drunk now, and very tired, but he had one last question. He looked at Algróinn and Vanadís.
"So may I take it that you are the rulers of Vanaheim?"
"We are not", replied Algróinn, "though you may be forgiven for thinking it. The rulers of Vanaheim, Laufgróðr and Grænlauf, live quiet, simple lives. Indeed, you have already met them. They are the couple with whom you spent a pleasant afternoon's gardening. They have been around for a very long time, and now choose to occupy themselves with unobtrusive, rustic pursuits."
Even more questions span in Snorri's head, but he could no longer pin them down and his eyes grew heavy. He felt he must already be partly dreaming, for the faces of his hosts were changing; they became foliate, with broad leaves where the cheeks, chin and eyebrows should have been. He fell forward onto the table, and the remains of his wine spilled across the board as the horn slipped from his hand.

When Snorri awoke, a greenish light pervaded the hall. He looked towards the window and saw that it was daylight, filtering through a heavy growth of greenery. He rose from the bed on which his hosts must have laid him after he had so indecorously fallen asleep, and rubbed his eyes. Looking about the hall, he saw that it, too, was filled with green growth. Vines entwined the columns and furniture, and the floor was bedecked with wild garlic and ground ivy. The soft bed on which he had lain was also one of leaves. No-one else was around, and he called out for Shiner with a rising sense of panic. No answer came. The environment that had previously been so warm and welcoming now felt oppressive and claustrophobic. Snorri staggered towards the door, crushing wild garlic underfoot and adding its pungent odour to the chlorophyl-scented air. He frantically pulled the door open, straining against the tendrils of bind and ivy that sought to hold it fast. The strands parted, and he saw Shiner holding the reins of Galdrafaxi and talking to Vaxandi. The pair looked on amused as Snorri disentangled himself from the rampant foliage.

"Nice of you to join us, Snorri", said Shiner, "we thought you might sleep all day. Come, we must be going, for there are other worlds to visit."

Snorri walked across to them through dewy, knee-high grass, and noticed that the plot where he had planted seedlings the previous afternoon now bore tall, flowering plants of a type he did not recognise. Shiner mounted and gave Snorri a hand up to sit behind him. Tall Vaxandi chose to walk, easily keeping up with long strides. From the yard at the back of the cottage, which now creaked under the weight of overgrowth, there came a shrill squeal. Snorri turned and glimpsed two large pigs, a boar and a sow. They were mating.

"Hm", Vaxandi quietly exclaimed. "I see that Uncle and Auntie haven't changed their routine. They always maintain that early morning is the best time for it."

All that morning, they ambled across the meadows of Vanaheim. Despite his earlier words, Shiner did not appear to be in any hurry, and he circumvented any woods that they encountered. Snorri's mind was so full of confusion that he hardly knew how to begin to frame a question. Eventually, Shiner seemed to realise his predicament, and informed him unbidden.

"What you saw at sunrise this morning was Vanaheim unleashed. It was explained to you last night that this is the realm from which all organic growth originates. It is most powerful, and even here it has to be kept in check. The Etins they hire don't come on until midday but, once they start, they work fast. The hall in which we dined will be restored to its attractive, tidy state soon, and the lord and lady who were our hosts will have assumed their regal appearance again. I have avoided the woodland because it is impassable at this time of day."

Snorri, still rather in shock at what he had witnessed, finally found the courage to give vent to his feelings.

"It was… the contrast. Yesterday afternoon, I lost myself in tending a garden and planting seedlings, work that I had only undertaken as a child, and had forgotten that I could enjoy. In the evening, we were entertained in courtly fashion by a lord and lady who wore the finest garb, and in a beautiful hall. Yet, just before I fell asleep, their faces changed to take on the look of the nature-demons that common folk believe in. And in the morning, everything was so full of wild-growth, and Vaxandi (he lowered his voice) intimated that his aunt and uncle had transformed into pigs."

Shiner nodded as the horse ambled on. "That is the paradox, dear Snorri. The Vanir are all these things at one and the same time. You mortals don't handle a paradox very well. You always assume that something must be one thing or another, and that the one is good and the other is bad. Perhaps it comes from the Christian teachings that you absorbed, of 'good' and 'evil', and you have trouble getting to understand the concept of balance. You love the spring and summer in Midgard, when all is growing and – all being well – it results in a good harvest; then you curse the autumn storms and the frosts that follow. You love the idea of lords and ladies in fine raiment, but you despise the pigs who farrow so abundantly and provide you with bacon. You love and simultaneously fear the Green Man of the woods, whose face you saw last night."

At this point, Snorri opened his mouth to protest, but Shiner sensed the protest and continued undaunted.

"Yes, you do. For all your Christian hypocrisy, you still honour the Green Man and the Corn-Goddess, and you love bacon. But has it ever occurred to you what it would be like if your all-growing spring carried on forever? Your pitiful houses and the palaces of your human rulers choked with everlasting growth, the orchards never pruned and hence failing to bear fruit? If the sow farrowed, but the blade never slaughtered, and you never tasted pork? You humans take on the role of the Etins in your own Midgard. Think about that."

Silence followed as they trotted on, with Snorri striving to absorb the lessons. They stopped at a hedge, and Shiner leaned down to shake Vaxandi's hand in farewell. Snorri was about to dismount, out of respect, to give his thanks, but Shiner bade him remain in his place.

"Farewell, Shiner! Farewell Snorri!", said Vaxandi. "You are the strangest visitor to have come to our fair realm. Can I not tempt you to stay? There is wine and meat a-plenty, and pleasant, peaceful work. Why venture any further?"

"Nice try, my friend", interjected Shiner, laughing. "Your charms might have worked, but I know all the counter-charms. Besides, Mister Snorri here still has much to learn, and I am bidden by a higher authority than yours to ensure that he attends his lessons."

Vaxandi laughed, waved, and then... simply disappeared. No, thought Snorri, not disappeared but transformed. Where he had stood, there was for a second a rich cloud of pollen that instantly drifted away on the breeze.

# Chapter 4 - Ljósálfheim

Shiner touched his spurs to Galdrafaxi's flanks, and again they rose skyward, initially into a bright blue vault, then beyond it into the greenish phosphorescence, and further along the now familiar broad white path of light that traversed the darkness. To Snorri, the journey seemed somehow shorter this time. Perhaps he was getting used to it, he thought. He certainly felt quite comfortable, and almost began to fancy himself an experienced traveller between the worlds. He felt rather more solid, in fact, and it occurred to him that Shiner had not offered any more of the sustaining mead, nor taken care that he was still wearing the torc. Leaning forward towards Shiner, he commented on this.
"I say, Shiner old boy, don't I need any more of that special mead to hold me together any longer?"
Shiner's response was a snort of laughter.
"Haha! For a mere mortal, and a dead one at that, you have certainly developed a taste for the beverages of Gods! I expect you were quite a boozer in your time on Earth."
Snorri paused, abashed, then continued.
"No... I didn't mean it like that. I'm not lusting for the stuff, tasty though it is. I'm just surprised that I feel fine now, and don't feel that I need it any more."
"You probably forgot that you consumed a belly-full of Vanic wine last night", Shiner said. "Your horn was replenished at least six times, to my certain knowledge. I'm surprised you don't have a hangover, or that you haven't turned all green and leafy!" He savoured the words once more. "Grrrreeennn and LEAFY!" And he laughed again as he continued.
"That gut-full of wine should see you through our next encounter. Hold it in fond memory – if you remember it – for you won't find anything like it on our next stop."

And then they were descending again, this time through an azure sky towards a bank of cumulus clouds. The air was clean and fresh as they approached the nearest cloud. It was a small cloud of shining white, an outlier, and on it lay a naked figure. It was masturbating. Snorri stared, goggle-eyed, but Shiner did not even deign to turn his head, and simply rode on. Soon they approached a towering castle composed entirely of cloud, shining bright and white in the sun. It had walls, towers, battlements and steeply-pitched roofs surmounted by streaming pennants of cirrus.

"I don't believe it!", gasped Snorri. "A real castle in the clouds! When I was a boy, I used to lie on the grass on fine summer days with my friends, and we speculated on who might live in those towering castles. I look forward to meeting its inhabitants!"

"Don't be deceived", growled Shiner. "It is but a show, put on to impress us because they knew we were coming. On a different day, we might have seen a whale, or a rhinoceros playing with a camel." Shiner's words meant nothing to Snorri. "A... what playing with a what?", he asked. Shiner hesitated, seeking an explanation. "Sorry", he said. "I meant a dragon playing with a horse." Snorri was still confused at first, then suddenly he understood. "Oh, yes, you mean the way the clouds change their shape. That was a constant source of amusement to us. First a whale, then a fisherman, a warrior, a reindeer, or some fantastic beast." He stared at the castle as if challenging it to change its shape, but they drew closer and it obstinately retained its form as they landed on the forecourt. Shiner dismounted and held out an arm to help Snorri dismount likewise, but Snorri hesitated. "Is it safe?", he asked. "It looks so insubstantial... a pavement of cloud. I fear I may fall through it." Shiner sighed.

"I assure you that it is as substantial as you are. You forget that you are the ghost of a man, held together by magic until this mission is accomplished. Now please alight, and let us get on with it."

Snorri sensed from Shiner's impatience that he had little taste for this place. His attitude stood in stark contrast to his cosy familiarity with Vanaheim the day before. Snorri's musings were, however, cut short by a deafening fanfare that issued from a tower. He jumped in surprise, and even Shiner appeared startled. Large doors opened in the castle's facade, and a shining apparition descended the steps leading down to the forecourt. The figure had the shape of a man, but it shone like the sun with an inner light. As it reached the bottom step, the brilliant light dimmed somewhat, so that Snorri was able to make out the form of a man with golden hair and very pale skin. He also saw that the man was entirely naked.

"Greetings, my Lord, and greetings to our guest!", the man exclaimed effulgently. "I am Alfrik, Steward of Light-Elf-Home, and it is our privilege to receive you!"

"Hail to you Alfrik", replied Shiner, "that was quite a welcome with the fanfare. How in the name of all that is holy did you manage that?"

The Elf simpered. "Oh, it was nothing, my Lord. A little borrowing from our dark cousins for the trumpets, a little practice, a little imagining. We desired to make an impression. Would you like to hear it again?" He raised an arm towards the tower, and the fanfare blared anew.

"NO!", shouted Shiner, then more calmly "no... thank you. Your welcome is much appreciated. Something... something more modest would be sufficient."

The radiant figure immediately gestured toward the tower with rapid, palms-outward hand movements and then a finger drawn across the throat. This was followed by another gesture with palms waved gently downward. Snorri caught the gestures as meaning 'Cut it out and tone it down'. The fanfare was instantly cut short and, after the briefest of pauses, was replaced by a tinny female voice singing a song. The language and the melody were strange to Snorri, but the lyrics filtered through to his ears as "If I knew you were coming I'd have baked a cake." Satisfied, Alfrik bade his guests follow him up the steps and into the castle. On each side of the high doorway stood an armed guard, but it appeared to Snorri that they were indistinct and faceless creatures of cloud and mist, projects begun but never quite completed. They were led into a banqueting hall, in the middle of which stood a long table with accompanying chairs. All of these were made of some twinkling, glassy substance. On the walls of the hall hung shields of an unusual, triangular shape.

Snorri tried to read the devices on the faces of the shields, but they constantly shifted. "Like clouds in the sky", Snorri thought.

The Steward of Light-Elf-Home graciously extended an arm to indicate that they should take a seat, and Snorri gingerly lowered himself onto one of the glassy chairs. To his surprise, it bore his weight adequately. He stared at Alfrik, still astonished at his nakedness. Alfrik must have read his mind for, the next time that Snorri glanced, he was clad decorously in a toga. Shiner sat also, and surveyed the decked table with a look that betrayed inevitable disappointment. There was meat and drink aplenty – roast goose, haunches of venison, goblets brimming with wine – but all of these were as glassy and transparent as the furniture.

After some fussing, Alfrik sat and declared "Honoured guests, please eat and drink your fill. It is but poor fare that we can offer here, but I pray you may enjoy it."

Snorri went to grasp a goblet. His hand passed through it, but he was starting to get the hang of strangeness in the worlds he was encountering. Focusing, he willed the goblet into solidity and was rewarded by the feel of cool, hard glass at his fingertips. He raised the glass, murmuring "May this wine be wholesome and quench my thirst", and then, as the rim of the goblet nearly touched his lips, remembered to ask Shiner "Is it safe to drink?"

Both Shiner and Alfrik were staring at him, agape. Snorri looked from face to face, unsure. "Well, is it?", he asked. Shiner was the first to respond, issuing an astonished breath from between pursed lips. "Pheeeeuw... but you learn fast, Mister Snorri. That magic took me years to learn. But yes, it is safe. Drink and eat all you will, and can, in this realm."

Snorri took a sip, and found the wine as flavourless as water and rather less substantial. In fact, it was rather like drinking cool, clear air. He drank the rest of the glass at a gulp, and the glass instantly refilled itself. Alfrik spoke again.

"I trust that you have had a pleasant journey thus far, Mister Snorri. We have looked forward to your arrival in this realm."

Snorri opened his mouth to reply, but it was Shiner who responded first.

"You may have looked forward to it, Alfrik, and I congratulate you on the pretty show you have put on, but the guards at the borders of your realm leave much to be desired. The one we encountered lay wanking on a cloud and did not even challenge us."

Alfrik stared blankly for a moment, then replied with a simpering smile and wave of his hand.

"The guards? Ah yes… the guards. Well, we do set them there more as a matter of protocol than anything else. After all, what would anyone steal from here? A thought? An idea? A few bars of music? A snatch of poetry? All of these things we give freely, as you know."

"Some of your ideas are damned dangerous, in my opinion", grumbled Shiner, "but perhaps I speak too much. It is for Snorri to ask questions and learn all he can of this kingdom."

Snorri did indeed have many questions, and Shiner's brusque interjection had given him time to frame some of them.

"Alfrik, you say you are the Steward of this realm, but who is its ruler?"

Alfrik smiled slyly and answered "Ah, Mister Snorri, are you testing me? You already know the answer to that. Ingvi-Frey is our ruler, thought we see little of him. An odd choice, to give the rulership of this Elf-home to a Wane, but who am I to question it?"

Snorri nodded, embarrassed. "Truly, it was a foolish question, but in a world of clouds and vapours I had to test whether there was some small fact that I could be sure of. Nothing here is as I expected, and I know nothing of the work and deeds of your people. You mentioned poetry, music and ideas: please tell me more."

Alfrik leaned back in his chair, literally puffing himself up with importance, for he visibly grew somewhat larger. "We do no work here", he said grandly, "all we do, we do for pleasure, though we need none of your coarse pleasures such as food and drink. Air and sunshine are all that we require."

"And wanking", muttered Shiner under his breath, thinking of the sentry.

"But of course", said Alfrik, who had caught the *sotto voce* comment, "does not sexual desire first begin in the mind? One might say that we govern all matters of the mind, and the more refined things that make the lives of mortals really worth living: poetry, music, great literature, invention, mathematics... even romance."

Snorri had been staring into his ever-full goblet, reflecting that some good, full-bodied, red wine would be preferable to a glass of air. Now he looked up at the Elf's luminous countenance.

"You say you govern poetry, and I consider myself something of an expert on that subject", he said. "Does not poetry come to the world of Men by virtue of the Holy Mead, which Odin won from the Etins?"

Alfrik laughed; a thin, sighing sound like a gust of wind.

"The Holy Mead! Yes, of course!", he chuckled, "but do you think it rains down upon you in unrefined form? You earthly poets would end up all wet and sticky! But I hear that you, Snorri, came to a sticky end. What? What?" And Alfrik laughed at his own joke, while Snorri remembered the pain of the cuts and the gushing of blood. He didn't find it a matter for joking.

Alfrik continued, unabashed.

"It is true that a trickle of that precious mead seeps down the bole of Yggdrasil from Asgard, but we, the Light Elves, distil it into a rarefied spirit that Men can easily absorb. We add a few thought-essences of our own – a metaphor here, a simile there – and then it is released to drizzle down on Midgard. Alas, it drizzles at random so that it is not always taken up by those best able to use it."

"And invention?", Snorri asked. "In Svartálfheim, the home of your earthier cousins, I saw some fine inventions, things that I would never have thought possible and could not fully understand. You surely cannot claim to have a monopoly of invention."

Alfrik snorted, whisps of mist issuing from his nostrils.

"Our dusky cousins do take on the... um... menial work of turning our inventions into practicable propositions", he said in a condescending tone, "but it is we who always provide the germ of the idea. We develop the ideal form, you see? But while our world is ideal, yours is far from it, so the ideal cannot be expressed as such in your imperfect world. The Dark Elves take the idea, turn it into a blueprint, and then it is usually forged in Midgard, though not always. Take, for example, Thor's hammer, the boar Gullinbursti, Freyr's ship Skiðblaðnir, or Odin´s spear Gungnir – wondrous things all; they were forged by Dwarfs, but we gave them the concepts!" Snorri nodded, considering, then replied.

"So you can't actually make anything yourselves."

Shiner turned his face away, but his shoulders shook, and Snorri knew he was laughing. Alfrik stuttered at first, then loftily began to declaim the perfection of the Light Elves' realm, and that material creation was below their dignity. Snorri was beginning to share Shiner's distaste for this conceited breed, with their airy castle of cloud and their table-fare which failed to satisfy. Sensing his advantage, he decided to press further.

"Steward Alfrik", he said in an earnest tone, "When I was in Svartálfheim, I saw Dwarfs unravel the soul-complex of dead humans, repurposing everything that surrounds the soul until nothing remained but the soul itself and the thin *hamr* that surrounded it. Then I saw other Dwarfs pop old souls into the heads of humans who were about to be born anew, giving them new life. I found that work most admirable. Can you do anything like that?"

Alfrik's head went from cumulus to cumulonimbus, becoming a dark, anvil-shaped thundercloud, though the eyes still shone brightly from within it. Lightning bolts showered from his crown to his shoulders.

"Oh YES!", he hissed, spitefully. "We can unravel a human mind, you'd better believe it! Some of our kind chose to cross the edge and dwell in your world of Midgard, which you fancy is the realm of Man. There they live in the woods and the rivers, and in the high, rocky places. They are the ones who grew bored of our perfect existence and developed a taste for mischief. They pick on travellers who traverse the deep, woodland paths and the mountain tracks, and they shoot elf-bolts at them to inflict disease or send them into madness." The Elf's external appearance had turned to a swirling vortex of dark red and purple as he warmed to his subject and revelled in the spite. "And I will tell you another thing, Snorri Sturluson: some of those souls you saw were Elf-souls, injected to live among humankind! Not all survive, for they are hampered by the unfamiliar, human body. Those of your time call them 'changelings'; others will have different names for them, but they are among you, and some of them – a few – are recognised for the genius they bring from Light-Elf-Home!"

There was a clap of thunder, a stormy gust, and the castle vanished. Snorri and Shiner found themselves sitting on a white cloud in bright sunshine. Shiner's horse, Galdrafaxi, was on another cloud, trying to graze but finding only puzzling disappointment. Shiner whistled to the horse and it galloped to them, easily crossing the intervening blue void. They mounted it, and Shiner spoke over his shoulder to Snorri.
"Quite a breed, aren't they, these Light Elves?"
"You can say that again!", Snorri replied with feeling. He sniffed, savouring the purity of the air, and continued.
"I hope there will be something better to eat and drink at our next stop."
"I warned you not to expect much", Shiner replied.
"Mind you", said Snorri, "there must have been something about their wine. I feel a poem coming on."

On another cloud, at the boundary between Ljósalfheim and Vanaheim, Alfrik was annoyed with himself. He had committed the cardinal sin, for a Light Elf, of becoming emotional. He, the Steward of the realm! He felt vengeful towards Snorri Sturluson and to that Shiner, but tried to dismiss the thought. That, too, was an emotion, and unworthy of him. Needing something, nevertheless, to rid himself of the self-loathing, he regarded the supine form of the sleeping sentry, and an idea came to him.
"Turn over, you bugger", he said.

# Chapter 5 – A magical interlude

Carried by Galdrafaxi's swift strides, Snorri and Shiner fared once more along the bright, broad path across the void. Snorri felt euphoric and became loquacious. All his initial trepidation was abandoned, and he was thoroughly enjoying the adventure.
"I say, Shiner, we certainly put that Elf in his place, didn't we? I can see why you don't like their kind. I always hated bluffers like that. All words and pretensions, airs and graces, like those skalds from Francia that I met. They would never have lasted five minutes in Iceland, where a man has to work hard for an honest living!"
"Well spoken, farm boy", Shiner replied, scornfully. "How many boulders did you have to shift to extend the home-acre? According to the biography handed to me before I began this mission, you were a privileged young punk who spent most of his early years in education."
Snorri was stung by the words, for they were largely true.
"Well, I didn't spend all my time at school", he said truculently, "at harvest I had to come home and help to mow the hay and the barley. And at the house-slaughter before Yule, I once slew a sheep!"
"Bully for you, great warrior", Shiner grinned, "but I think you may have earned yourself some lasting enemies from our recent encounter. You should watch your back in your next life, and look for other sources of inspiration if you wish to be a poet again."

Snorri had to ponder on Shiner's words for several minutes, and his exuberant loquacity was stilled. The mention of enemies reminded him of the injudicious involvement in politics that had led to his death. But, more importantly now, there was that mention of his next life. What next life? He had fancied that, since he had been told that he was not destined for Hell, he would survive all these adventures and then come to sit on the right hand of God. Forever. Now he was being told that there might be another life in which he would have enemies and, furthermore, might desire to be a poet again, and need inspiration from a source that he had slighted. It all took some digesting, and not a little worry. They rode on in silence across the inky void until Snorri noticed that Galdrafaxi was slowing to a trot, then a walk.

"Are we stopping?", asked Snorri. "Why are we stopping?"

Shiner said nothing. He brought the horse to a halt and dismounted. With a motion of his head, he indicated that Snorri should also dismount. Alarmed, Snorri demurred. There was nothing on which to stand but the broad belt of light. Seeing his hesitation, Shiner shrugged and made a sweeping wave of his hand. A round patch of grass, perhaps a dozen yards in diameter, appeared to one side of the shining road, and Shiner led the horse onto it by the reins.

"Does that make you feel better?", he asked. "I can add some refinements if you like." He wiggled the fingers of his right hand; daisies appeared among the grass, and the patch was surrounded by a low growth of hawthorn. Birdsong filled the air. Snorri reluctantly dismounted.

"A pretty illusion", he conceded, "and I know that it is only illusion, but I thank you for its comfort. But you still haven't told me why we have stopped."

Shiner was busy unloading some items from a saddle bag, and he spoke without turning.

"The next place that we are to visit is the most dangerous of all, and I must make preparations. All that I require of you is silence."

Snorri watched as Shiner laid the items before him among the grass and daisies. There was a wand, a small sack, a leather bottle, two bowls, and an earthen vessel, on the outside of which frost had formed. Into one of the bowls he poured soil from the sack, into the other water from the bottle. When he had done this, Shiner stood in silence for a moment, head bowed. He shrugged his shoulders a couple of times and gently shook his arms as they hung at his sides, willing his body into relaxation. His breathing became long, deep and steady, and Snorri fancied he saw twinkling specks of blue light appearing and disappearing all over Shiner's tall form. Behind them, Galdrafaxi cropped the grass and seemed to find it satisfying. Finally, Shiner raised his arms up, forward and back in an encompassing gesture, and a sphere of sky-blue light surrounded the entire islet. Then, taking up the wand, he raised an arm above his head; a pool of brilliant, white light suddenly materialised above them, brighter by far than the shining road. Its light illuminated the grassy platform like a lightning flash, every blade of grass etched out starkly and casting a shadow. Shiner's hand descended, drawing down the light to the crown of his head, then his throat and his solar plexus. He uttered the words "Vé – Óðinn – Vili!" as he did so, then the hand came up to the right shoulder and across to the left with the words "Huginn – Muninn!". All of these names Snorri recognised. They were the names of Odin and his brothers, and of the two ravens that sat on Odin's shoulders. A cross of light had formed on, and within, Shiner, and Snorri watched as it transformed into Mjölnir, the hammer of Thor, but Shiner had only just begun. Now he circled on the spot, his wand tracing runes on the circumference of the blue sphere. They glowed with a piercing and powerful red light. Many of them Snorri recognised, but instead of the familiar sixteen, there were twenty-four, and eight of them he did not know. He now felt very small as he continued to observe the spectacle; Shiner, conversely, seemed to have grown to gigantic proportions as he concluded this rite, casting an unfamiliar rune at each quarter, and above and below them. Snorri kneeled and focused on the bright-lit grass, overwhelmed by the immense power that had been gathered. When he dared to look up again, the vision made him gasp. Shiner, his irascible, scornful, humorous but protective guide and travelling companion was gone, to be replaced by an image of sheer might. The humanity had vanished, and he appeared god-like. The Hammer of Thor shone clearly in his upper body, and the runes of the perimeter shone their rays inwards to the centre that he embodied, forming a swirling vortex of red, black and white power. His eyes glowed red, and flames issued from his mouth as he uttered chants in a language that Snorri could not understand. He took the bowl of earth and sprinkled the soil around the edge of the circle, and some of it on Snorri. Then he took the frosted, earthenware vessel and poured its contents into the bowl of water, speaking runes as he did so. The water boiled and a freezing vapour poured down from it as the spoken runes hung, shining, in the air. Most were incomprehensible, though Snorri saw the rune that meant 'Ice' over and over again, and it was always an icy blue. Shiner stood up, and his cloak and outer raiment were gone. He stood naked, dipping his fingers into the bowl and tracing the ice-rune onto the several parts of his body. He turned to Snorri and, in a commanding tone, said "Strip!" Snorri had no option but to obey, and his fingers pulled at his tunic, only to go straight through it, for it was spun of the magic that held him together after death.

"Never mind", said the towering, naked Shiner. He waved his wand and Snorri, too, stood naked. Shiner again dipped his fingers into the bowl and traced runes on Snorri's head, torso and limbs. The runes burned cold, like frostbite, and they glowed ice-blue. Shiner turned away and similarly anointed Galdrafaxi. The horse quivered and trembled at the touch of the freezing glyphs, but remained calm. There followed a long chant from Shiner, his voice sometimes rising and roaring like a storm, at other times whispering like a breeze and barely audible. At the end, he spread his arms and uttered words that Snorri recognised, for they were the final verse of the Hávamál, the Lay of the High One.

"Now are High-One's words spoken,
In High-One's Hall!
Useful to the sons of men,
But of no use to Etin sons.
Hail to the one who spoke them!
Hail, to the one who knows them!
Useful, to the one who took them.
Hail, to those who hear them!"

Shiner then staggered across to Galdrafaxi and leaned against the saddle, his head resting on his forearms. He looked spent, and stood thus for a long time. The Thor's Hammer image and the vortex of red, black and white dissipated but did not leave the shining, blue sphere. Indeed, they added to it and appeared to enhance it with their energy. After many long minutes, Shiner recovered, and the customary clothing reappeared to cover his nakedness.

"Get dressed", he said abruptly. Snorri surveyed his limbs, on which the icy runes still glowed brightly.

"How?", he asked.

"In the same way that you made Alfrik's wine potable", Shiner replied. "Will it. Just will it." Snorri understood, and thought of the clothes in which he wanted to be clad. His ghost had previously worn the clothes in which he had died, hiding from assassins in his bathroom; those had still borne gashes from sword-strokes. Now he invented for himself a fine raiment, the best he had ever worn in the courts of kings, with intricate embroidery in filigree of gold. All of it was brought instantly into manifestation by the simple wish. He watched in silence as Shiner diligently packed all of the magical items back into the saddle bags, and noticed that the grassy island on which they stood was gradually fading and becoming less distinct. While it still held, Shiner completed the packing and approached Snorri again, leading Galdrafaxi by the reins.

"Snorri Sturluson", he said in a solemn tone, "I did not know the purpose of the mission that has been entrusted to me, and I still do not fully understand it. I must guide the ghost of an insignificant mortal among the eight outer worlds, and ensure that he learns something of them. Your conduct so far has impressed me, but you must know…" Snorri opened his mouth, about to express his thanks for the compliment, but Shiner cut him short. "But you must know that the next stage of our journey is the most dangerous undertaking. We are about to visit a realm that I have myself only ever viewed from a distance. Were it up to me, I would not venture there at all, but take you I must. I bid you hold your tongue, and speak when you are spoken to. Be respectful, for the being we are about to meet can snuff out your existence in a trice. ALL of it, do you understand? Even your soul would cease to exist!"

# Chapter 6 – Muspelsheim

"If it is so dangerous", Snorri quailed, "then why should we go there? You have shown me so many wonders already. I did not ask for this, and I do not wish to endanger you. Can we not omit this part, and proceed to pleasanter worlds?"
Shiner bowed his cloaked head.
"No, we cannot omit it. It is commanded, both for you and for me. We can but obey. Now mount up, for the pleasant island that I created for you is disintegrating. Be confident, above all. I have expended much magic to ensure that we will be safe and protected."
Head still bowed, he tapped his thigh with his fingers for a moment and seemed to be trying to remember something. Then it came back to him.
"Those glasses you were given in Vanaheim, do you still have them?"
Snorri reached into the ornate and bejewelled pouch that he had imagined for himself. To his amazement, the glasses were inside it. He held them out to Shiner, who simply passed a hand over them. The transparent lenses became coal-black and completely opaque. Trying them on again, Snorri could see nothing at all through them.
"They will protect your eyes against the brightness we will meet", said Shiner. They mounted Galdrafaxi, and the horse trotted forward at the touch of Shiner's heels. Looking back over his shoulder, Snorri saw the island of green become transparent, break into fragments, and then disappear altogether. The blue sphere that Shiner had cast persisted, however, and moved with them, continuing to surround them.

The pace increased to a gallop, and the horse and its riders sped again along the shining white road. Ahead of them, a brighter light appeared in the distance and quickly grew in intensity as they approached. Snorri put on the black glasses and found that he could still see it through them.
"Is that… is that the sun?", he asked.

Shiner snorted derisively.

"Ha! No, my friend, that is the gateway to Muspelsheim, the realm of primal fire, of which the sun is but a spark."

The eye-searing apparition enlarged rapidly as the distance diminished, revealing itself as an elliptical gateway to a world of light and flame. At the point when it almost filled Snorri's vision, Shiner reined in the horse and waited in silence. From the surging inferno emerged a gigantic, man-shaped figure, itself composed of licking tongues of flame. Even with the glasses on, Snorri could barely stand to look at its brightness, and he had to raise a hand and peer between his fingers. The heat was tremendous, and without the magical shield spun by Shiner they would have been burned to nothing in a second. A deafening voice boomed like the eruption of a volcano.

"WHO DARES TO APPROACH MY DOMAIN?"

Shiner, who had the hood of his cloak pulled forward to cover most of his face, replied.

"Lord Surt, I come in the name of High-One, Odin, the Allfather, to request a boon on his behalf."

Rumbling continued, the breathing of a giant, as Surt considered this.

"Odin... Odin... yes, I think I remember that name. Did he not commit a murder and then build mud pies out of the victim's corpse a short while ago? What does the young upstart want from me?"

Shiner steeled himself to make the request, knowing that a wrong word might result in annihilation.

"Lord Surt, he sends greetings and requests only that you deign to impart a little knowledge to the ghost of a mortal. It is but a small thing, and it may be that we can do you a small favour in return."

Blasting laughter was the response, causing sparks and jets of flame to erupt from the gateway. Gadrafaxi shifted nervously, but the flames and sparks fell harmlessly against the shielding blue sphere. Snorri felt more afraid than he had ever thought possible, but he remembered Shiner's encouraging words, *"Be confident, above all"*, and forced himself to have faith that they would come through the encounter unscathed. The thunderous voice rang out again.

"Fools! You are beneath contempt! Do you not know that I am The Ancient? I was there before your beginning. I *am* the beginning! I, together with my sister Jökulheið. What care I for Odin's grubs? Your puny minds could not hold even a tiny part of all the knowledge that I hold."

Shiner persisted, employing all the diplomacy that he could muster. "You speak truth, oh Lord", he said. "Mortal humans have heard the name of Surt, but they are quite unable to comprehend your might. They think in terms of the heat of the sun, and of the fires that issue from the bowels of the earth when a volcano erupts. They really have no conception. For example, this man-ghost, whom I am commanded to instruct, mentioned you in a book while he was alive on Midgard. He thinks that you wish nothing more than to destroy all life and all of Odin's creation, but are held in check for now. Indeed, they believe much foolish nonsense. I am sorry to waste your time in this way, but I was commanded thus."

A fresh gush of flame spewed from the gateway as Surt snorted. "Time? Waste my time? What know you of time? I have seen aeons pass, and I am timeless."

Shiner lowered his head in a gesture that he hoped would be interpreted correctly, a nod of humble appreciation. His ruse was working and, despite the anticipated scorn, he was beginning to elicit information from this lord of primaeval fire.

"Let me see the man-ghost", said Surt, and Shiner leaned to his right so that the flame-giant could see Snorri more clearly. Surt looked down from his tremendous height and saw a pale, terrified face, the eyes covered by black discs that reflected his own incandescence.

"What does it wear over its eyes?", Surt asked. "The eyes are the windows of the soul, and I want to see its soul. Make it take the black shields away."

"My Lord", Shiner replied evenly, "I could do that, but it is inadvisable. Your brightness would burn out his eyes in an instant, rendering him blind. And then he would not be able to look upon the fair countenance of Jökulheið."

To his satisfaction, Shiner noted that his words had the desired effect. Surt was stunned, and for several moments, which to the terrified Snorri seemed like an age, there was only the rumble of his breathing, though that was as loud as any volcano. Finally, Surt spoke again.

"You... intend to see my sister? When? How?"

"The next stage of our journey will take us to Niflheim", said Shiner, "if this grub, as you describe him, can survive the journey. I agree that he is a puny thing, unworthy of your consideration."

But Surt hardly appeared to hear him, lost in his own musings.

"It has been so long since I saw Jökulheið, Glacier-Bright", he sighed. "She and I are the First, brother and sister, and lovers. The last time we met, I looked across the void which you call Ginnungagap, and again I was overwhelmed by her beauty. We reached out to each other across the gap, and we mated, fire and ice. Our union gave birth to a wonderful creation that filled up the gap. We had many children, some hot and bright like me, others cold and mysterious like her. You say that this man-ghost believes that I am set upon destroying his world? Why?"

"Indeed, Lord", replied the cunning Shiner smoothly. "It is said in some prophecy they have that Surt and his sons, together with frost-giants, will rage across heaven and earth, trampling all in their path and annihilating men and Gods alike."

Surt's eyes flashed so brightly that Shiner saw the light through the hood of his magic-imbued cloak, and Snorri hid his head behind Shiner's shoulders.

"Utter nonsense!", Surt bellowed, and a fresh gale of flame surrounded the blue sphere.

"She and I will meet again at the allotted time, and our mating will be a thing of beauty. If worlds are destroyed, it is merely because they get in our way. Those worlds are transient things, but we are eternal, and our procreation will give rise to new worlds. Brief mortals and their petty Gods should not concern themselves with this."

Surt's light seemed to dim a little as he continued, sadly.

"In any case, it will be aeons yet before our mating. Mortals and Gods alike should occupy themselves in making what happiness they can find. There is nothing they can do to prevent us coming together when the time is ripe."

Shiner felt that Snorri had obtained as much as he could have expected, and more, from this dangerous interview.
"We thank you, Lord Surt, for your patience. Now we must be on our way again, for we still have four worlds to visit."
"Will you be paying a visit to Asgard?", asked Surt.
"Yes, of course", Shiner replied.
"Then tell that young pup Odin that he wastes his time collecting his dead warriors, the Einherjar, in the hope of stopping my sister and me coming together again. By the way, what is the name of your man-ghost? If he is so important to Odin, I should perhaps have cause to remember him."
"His name was Snorri Sturluson in life" said Shiner, "though I do not know how he may be called in his next life."
"Show him to me again", commanded Surt, and Shiner leaned sideways again to reveal Snorri sitting upright on the horse.
"Snorri Sturluson", Surt said, "since you are to meet my sister – something I cannot do yet – then please bring her a gift from me, that she may remember me and know that I love her."
Snorri felt the weight of his pouch increase slightly, and then Shiner was turning Galdrafaxi away to face another light-road. Snorri turned his head, daring to look at Surt as he stood in Muspelsheim's gate, and he thought he saw a bright tear of lava trickle down the giant's cheek. He silently projected a thought: "Trust me; I will deliver it, with your love."

Galdrafaxi cantered northward along the shining path, relieved to be away from that hot place. The blue sphere that had shielded them flared for a moment and disappeared. Shiner released a sigh of relief.
"Well, that went much better than expected. I hope you picked up a lot of knowledge from that. I certainly did."

Snorri said nothing. He was looking into his pouch to see what Surt had placed there, and drew it out. It was a dry ear of bracket fungus, the kind of fungus that forms little 'elf-seats' on the trunks of dying birch trees. In a small hollow on its surface glowed an ember, the keepsake from a fire-giant to his sister-lover. Snorri blew on the ember and vowed not to let it die.

Shiner was in a good mood. He allowed Galdrafaxi to continue at his own pace, which was an easy trot, and for once was conversational as they rode. Snorri had slipped the bracket fungus with its burning ember back into his pouch, but he continued to mull on Surt's words. A brother and sister who were also lovers: it seemed unnatural, but what else should these beings of fire and ice call themselves? They were, as Surt had said, the First, pre-existing everything – even the Etins, the Aesir and the Vanir. They had mated at the beginning of all things, thereby spawning everything that was familiar, even in mythology. They would mate again, Surt had said, and in their joining would sweep away all of that away. It was nothing personal, but it was not impersonal either, for to Surt and Jökulheið it meant the height of joy. He found he could sympathise with them, enduring loneliness for aeons between their periodic copulations, and he wondered how many times they had already mated, how many universes they had already generated and then destroyed. His thoughts were interrupted as he became aware that Shiner had been speaking to him.
"I'm sorry", he said, "what did you say?
Shiner turned in the saddle and spoke again. He was smiling.
"I said, are you looking forward to seeing Midgard again?"
Snorri was taken aback, and it took him a few seconds to make the mental adjustment.
"Midgard? We are going to Midgard? I thought I already knew that world."
"No choice", Shiner replied. "Our route so far has been a round-about one, but Midgard lies directly between Muspelsheim and Niflheim. We must either go around it or go through it, and to go

through it is quicker by far. Besides, I think you may find that there is far more to Midgard than you could ever have known."

# Chapter 7 – Midgard

They rode on for a while until a fuzzy, hazy tangle of light came into view, an orb of shining threads that reminded Snorri of the webs spun by some species of spider. It expanded as they grew closer, and now he could see shining roads like the ones they had been travelling, all converging at the orb. Shiner reined in the horse and turned again in the saddle. With a sweep of his arm, he explained the sight before them.
"All roads lead to Midgard, one might say. It is the great junction, the prime node of Yggdrasil. That is why it is called the Middle-Enclosure, or Middle-Earth. That road", he pointed out, "leads westward to Vanaheim, where we have already been. Its counterpart leads east to Jötunheim, Etin-home, which we have yet to visit. The road we now travel, from Muspelsheim, continues on past Midgard, north to Niflheim; you cannot see it now because Midgard stands in the way. That shining column stretching up and down comes from Asgard above, through Light-Elf-Home, and after Midgard extends downward to Dark-Elf-Home, which you have also seen, and to Hel, where we began our journey. There are other roads, of course, connecting these worlds by more circuitous routes, but Midgard is the place where all roads meet."
Snorri was impressed and, at the same time, baffled.
"I had not expected our little world to be so important", he said. "I told people about the old beliefs, about the Gods and wights that you have introduced me to, and I was myself enchanted by the old stories, but the priests taught me that our world – my old world – is a poor kind of place; a place of trial and suffering, on which we live our brief lives until we may, after we die, live in Heaven. Or be cast down into a place of eternal punishment if we do not obey the Lord's commandments. But already, with the many things you have shown me, I now know that it is far from as simple as that. However, I still do not fully comprehend this."
Shiner reached around to pat Snorri's shoulder in a gesture of comfort and unprecedented familiarity, and bared his teeth again in that now-familiar snarl of a smile.

"Don't worry", he said, "it is a lot to take in, and even more to explain. Let us trot on, and things may become clearer."
He touched his heels to Galdrafaxi's flanks and they moved on to the edge of the orb and into it. The shining threads resolved themselves into beads of light, and then the beads resolved themselves into spiralling wheels, each composed of trillions of stars. Between the wheels and the stars, dark clouds of black matter sometimes intervened, and Shiner sometimes steered Galdrafaxi with his knees to avoid a hole of blackness. Snorri surveyed all of this in astounded silence. On clear nights, when he had lived, he had sometimes seen what was called the Milky Way, seeing it so clearly that he had felt he could reach up, grasp it, and tug it down, but this was a hundred times as clear, and it all had colour: reds, blues, greens, and colours that he could not even name. Yet he was puzzled. Where was the anticipated flat, green disc of Midgard, surrounded by ocean? He was impatient to see it, and asked Shiner.
"This is all very beautiful", he said, but I don't see Midgard yet. Only stars."
Shiner nodded.
"As I told you, there is more to Midgard than you could have ever known. All of this is Midgard. It is the realm of physical existence, of manifest reality, and by the scale of Man's imagining it is huge in itself. What did you expect? A flat, green plate, surrounded by Ymir's eyebrows?"
Snorri did not know what to say at first, for Shiner seemed to have read his thoughts, but he gave an honest answer.
"Yes, I must admit that I expected that. With a curtain of stars surrounding it, and the sun and moon revolving around it. I try to discern it, but I cannot see it here among all these stars and these... these clusters of stars. Midgard is... was... my home, but I do not recognise this as home. Where has it gone to?"
Shiner nodded again and said:
"I understand. I cannot show you the flat world that you thought Midgard to be, but I can show you something close."

And with that, he urged Galdrafaxi on again through the starscape until they approached one of those spiralling wheels that held many stars, aiming for the edge of one particular curving spoke. On and downwards they galloped. Or was it upwards? Snorri had lost his sense of orientation in this vastness, and wisely decided that it did not matter. Eventually they neared a star. It was quite a small one, of a yellowish colour, and it had a number of bodies that circled around it, some quickly, some slowly. Those that were nearer the star appeared to revolve more quickly. They passed a ring of small rocks and a small, round body that reflected the star's rays with a reddish colour, until Shiner reined Galdrafaxi to a walk, keeping pace with a sphere that looked blue and white on the side which faced the star. It reminded Snorri of a bead of coloured glass that he had once treasured as a small boy, and for some unaccountable reason he felt homesick. He noticed also that a tiny, grey orb circled this pretty globe.

"Can we go in closer?", he asked. "For some reason I feel drawn to this shiny, blue-and-white marble."

"You should", Shiner replied, "for this was your world, and you considered it to be the whole of Midgard." And with those words, they swooped down for a closer look. Snorri saw seas, clouds and land masses, and noted that the globe was turning on its axis so that all of these features were at times exposed to the light from the star and at other times in darkness. The little grey orb steadily moved around it, also exposed by turns to the light from the star: sometimes a crescent, then half-exposed, then fully reflecting the star's light.

"Just like the phases of Máni", he whispered to himself. Then he also noticed that the horse's movements had become frozen in time, and that Shiner had not shifted his position for some seconds. Indeed, his own thought processes seemed to slow; he found it hard to maintain a train of thought, as though he had become an old dotard. No sooner had the thought occurred to him, than Galdrafaxi was galloping away again. The blue marble and the star that it circled receded into the distance.

"Hey", he protested. "Why are we off so soon?" I should have liked to examine that little world more closely!"

"Of course you would", Shiner replied as they galloped on, "for that was the tiny part of Midgard that you understood in your life. You were naturally drawn to it, but for various reasons we had to move on."

Snorri still felt indignant, but Shiner spurred Galdrafaxi until stars flew past them in a blur. It was like looking into a downfall of hail. They did not stop until they were on the other side of the system and looking back into it. They halted, on the bright road again.

"Let's dismount and give Galdrafaxi a breather", said Shiner. "Do you require a grassy island again, or do you feel more confident on the road this time?"

Snorri would have liked a pasture under his feet, however illusory, but felt that this was a challenge to his courage. He swallowed his nervousness and, refusing Shiner's proffered arm, stepped down onto the road. To his relief, it felt quite solid. Shiner unsaddled the horse and allowed it to move around freely. It looked for grass, and then, disappointed, rolled for a while on the road, laid down, and went to sleep. Snorri demanded again to know why he had not been allowed to see more of the globe that attracted him so. Shiner had been rummaging in one of the saddlebags, checking its contents, but now he stopped and faced Snorri.

"Felt homesick, didn't you?", he said. It was more a statement than a question, and Snorri admitted that it was so.

"That was one reason to leave. Your spirit might have been drawn down to it, and you would have become a wandering phantom, forever seeking the places that used to be familiar to you; ineffectual and lost in morose nostalgia. Is that what you would want?"

Snorri shook his head, and Shiner continued.

"Another reason was that time was affecting us. Did you not feel it? And we were affecting time as long as we lingered there. Midgard is the realm of causality, the only world that is ruled by time as you know it. Four hundred years passed while we were crossing it."

Snorri struggled to understand it, gave up, and raised another subject instead.

"You told me that the little, blue-and-white globe was my world, everything that I had thought of as Midgard. I see now that it is an orb, and not flat as I had previously thought, but I cannot get over how insignificant it is among all vastness that you tell me is the whole of Midgard. I thought our earth was big, and that the stars were tiny points of light surrounding it. Now I see that it is the other way round. Four hundred years, you said? How brief our mortal lives must seem to the Gods! I am surprised they notice us at all. So why do we humans devote so much time, give so many offerings, and strive to obey beings who can barely even notice that we exist?"

Shiner looked into Snorri's eyes. He wondered for a moment whether he ought to reveal such a mystery to this poor man-ghost, then remembered his orders that nothing should be held back. Besides, he was, despite himself, beginning to like Snorri, and to admire his quick intelligence.

"Midgard is but one of the nine worlds", he said. "Your little globe is spatially but a miniscule part of it, but do not underestimate its significance. That little orb, the world of Man, is the chess-board, and the Gods themselves envy the urgency of your brief, mortal lives. All the other worlds act upon Midgard, playing out their games of combat and co-operation. As well as humans, Dwarfs and elves live there, and Gods project their avatars to live among you. They love to witness your mortality. The game gives them purpose and inspiration and, besides, your belief in them strengthens them via the avatars that they project. They need that belief; it is food and drink to them."

Snorri pondered Shiner's words. Many words were strange to him, but he thought he understood the concept, and he felt sullen and used.

"So we are the playthings of the Gods? And we feed them with our belief? What if we simply stopped believing? Would they leave us alone, and allow us to simply get on with our lives?"

"They might", Shiner replied, "but it is a symbiotic relationship. You need the Gods – and the Dwarfs, the Elves, and the Etins – as much as they need you. Without the Vanir, no crop could grow. Without the Etins, who sweep away the overgrowth, the crops would be overwhelmed by wild growth of weeds and pests. Without the Elves, you would have no ideas, arts, invention or writing. Without the Dwarfs you would have no ploughs, swords or other tools. And without the Aesir, you would eventually lose your consciousness and your own sense of purpose. Your world would decay, and with it all the other worlds. Yggdrasil would become a bare, leafless tree."

Snorri was silent as he tried to digest the enormity of all that Shiner had revealed to him. Though it completely went against his Christian upbringing, he had to admit that it made sense. After all, did it make any more sense to live a life of suffering because of something that the first humans had unwittingly done, earning the punishment of a vengeful God? And then to grovel and obey, in the hope of being admitted to a tedious Heaven, where nothing ever changed and there was neither day nor night, and trees simultaneously blossomed and bore fruit; fruit that you could never enjoy, because you were too busy singing praises to that vengeful Lord? Shiner watched silently, trying to read Snorri's thoughts and having a great deal of success. But Snorri was not yet done. He had another question.
"You used that word… 'avatar'. What does it mean?"
Shiner considered how to describe it.
"It is a projection. Gods cannot literally live on the earth, so they make projections of themselves that humans can understand. These projections form the medium through which Gods and men can communicate. They have to take a form that humans can understand."
Snorri did not understand, and said so, so Shiner continued.
"You have been a lover, a husband, a father, and a poet to kings", he said. "How did you project yourself in each of these roles?"

"That's easy", Snorri said. "When I was a lover, I was brash, and showed off those aspects of myself that might win the heart of a young woman. As a husband, I was dutiful but stern, and I tried to be discreet in my philandering. As a father, I was firm but loving. And at the courts of kings, I tried to be wise and dignified. Does that answer your question?"
Shiner nodded.
"Yes, it does. In each of the roles that you played, you projected an avatar according to the occasion. A face that was you, but not the whole of you. Did you ever expose your doubts and worries, your lack of self-esteem, or tell that you pissed your bed until you were nine years old?"
Snorri did not know what to say. Clearly, there was altogether too much in the biography that Shiner had been given, so he remained silent as Shiner went on.
"You see, the Gods project a form of themselves upon Midgard that humans can understand. When humans lived at one with nature, these were often animal forms. In your writings, for example, you describe Odin as eagle-headed, or accompanied by wolves and ravens. But for your ancestors, he *was* the eagle, the raven and the wolf. Later, these avatars took on human form, but with animal heads and, later still, they were seen in entirely human form but accompanied by the animals that they had once been. In your time on earth you saw him as a traveller of middle age, with a cloak and a floppy hat. Now, in Midgard, it is four hundred years later. Who knows what form he may take now? Gods have to change their avatars so that humans can keep up. Like you, they do not project the whole of their beings. They project the image that they wish."

Shiner clearly deemed the lesson to be at an end, for he resumed his check of the saddlebag's contents. A thought occurred to him. "What did Surt give you?", he asked Snorri. "He mentioned a gift, a keepsake."
Snorri drew the dry fungus and its ember from his pouch and showed it. Shiner gave a low whistle.

"Fire from Muspelsheim!", he exclaimed. "We can certainly use that where we are going, a place which may prove no less dangerous. Give it to me!"

"No", Snorri replied flatly.

Shiner's jaw dropped for a second, then he recovered himself.

"You must give it to me, Snorri", he insisted, "I need its magic to help keep us safe."

"No", Snorri repeated. "It was entrusted to me, to bear to Niflheim and give to Jökulheið. This I will do."

Shiner's face was set hard now, and Snorri could see that he was angry.

"I could make you give it to me", Shiner said.

"Perhaps you could", Snorri replied, growing angry himself at this bullying, "but that would bring an end to my co-operation. I would not take a step further, and your mission would have failed. How would that sound when you report back to your boss?"

Shiner paced in a circle, angrily kicking at the road of light, which obstinately refused to throw up any pebbles or sparks. Galdrafaxi woke and stood up, giving an uneasy whinny. A wand appeared in Shiner's outstretched hand, pointing at Snorri.

"For the last time, Snorri, just give me the damned thing, or I shall carve runes to curse you. I will not be disobeyed!"

It was too much for Snorri, and he gave full vent to all the confusion and frustration that he had endured on the journey so far.

"Well fucking do it then!", he roared. "Do you think I care? I'm dead, a fucking man-ghost, am I not? Just a shade with imagined clothes and a swig of magic mead to keep him going. What's the worst that can happen to me? I'm sick of being pushed around: 'Snorri mount up!'; 'Snorri dismount!'; 'Snorri mind your manners!'. I didn't ask for this, and I'm tired of it all."

He put his head back and laughed mirthlessly.

"You know, the only one who has treated me with any civility since this all began, the only one who said 'please' to me, was a cosmic fire-giant who could have stripped my soul away. So yeah, I'm taking this ember to Niflheim, and I'll hand it over in person. If you try to stop me, I'll find a way back to Surt somehow, and you will have to explain to him why his gift didn't reach the recipient. Maybe he'll get so angry at that that he'll bring forward the liaison, and you can say goodbye to your entire shit-show!"

Snorri stood, panting after his outburst, a fire worthy of Surt himself burning in his eyes.

Shiner was speechless, completely deflated, and his arms hung at his sides. When he eventually spoke again, all his suaveness and authority were gone.

"You would really do that?", he asked. Snorri trembled now with the aftershock that follows profound emotion, but he was still stubbornly determined.

"You can bet your immortal soul on it", he replied, then sank to sit on the road, knees drawn up.

Shiner stood for a long while, staring at him, then moved to sit down next to Snorri. Silence reigned for an earthly decade or two until Shiner spoke again.

"I'm sorry", he said. "I own that I have been pushing you around a lot. Command becomes a habit, and a bad one at that, if we forget that others have their own feelings and aims. I won't ask you for the fire again. We can manage without it."

Snorri just nodded, exhausted by the episode. He looked up to view the white road ahead, and then back over his shoulder to the misty, orb spider's web that was Midgard, and felt tired and lonely. He began to wish for the peace of the grave, to simply sleep. He pictured himself being dismantled by those kindly Dwarfs until nothing was left but an outline and a small light in the depths of Hel. His head nodded toward his chest, and wisps of his being started to come loose, faintly glowing filaments that drifted from his ghost and wafted away into the ether. He was brought back by a hard thump against his shoulder and Shiner's voice.

"Snorri! SNORRI! Please wake up and drink this!"

He awoke, and groggily saw the leather bottle that was held before his face. He didn't really want to wake up, but accepted the bottle anyway and took a swig. Everything came back into focus. He was still on the shining road, with six worlds behind him and unknown challenges ahead. Taking another swig, he remembered that he had

a promise to keep, blew again on the ember, and returned the fungus to his pouch.
"Hey", he said, "you said 'please'."

# Chapter 8 – Niflheim

Midgard faded into the distance behind them as Galdrafaxi and his two riders sped along the road. It was getting colder, and Snorri shivered. Frost formed on his beard and moustache, and stung the tip of his nose. The aurora that he had seen on the way to Vanaheim formed again. It was no longer only green, however, but composed of many different hues including red, yellow and violet. He recalled the aurora, the *norðrljós* or northern light, above Iceland when he had been alive, and he remembered the bone-chilling winter nights when it was usually visible. It felt like a message and a promise of the cold to come. Before Niflheim came into view, Shiner brought Galdrafaxi to a halt.
"Come, Snorri", he said, "let us dismount and make the necessary preparations."
He swung a leg over the horse's neck and slid down, but Snorri remained in his place behind the saddle, looking ahead.
Shiner looked up at him, puzzled, and assumed Snorri was still smarting because of his earlier peremptory tone.
"Um, I mean, *please* would you dismount so that we can get on with this?", he said.
Snorri didn't move. Still looking ahead, he replied.
"We don't need to do this."
Shiner's thick eyebrows knitted in bafflement.
"Really? Are you saying that we don't need to visit Niflheim? I can assure you that it forms an essential part of your education. We have visited Muspelsheim, and to balance it you must… need to… visit its opposite. And what about your promise to deliver Surt's gift?"
Snorri still did not move except to slowly turn his head to face Shiner.
"No", he said. "I don't mean that. I mean that you don't need to make preparations. At least, not exactly in the way you did before we went to Muspelsheim."
Shiner gave a derisive snort. Part of him wanted to simply pull Snorri from Galdrafaxi's back, but he was learning to respect his

stubbornness and forced himself to adopt a more diplomatic approach.

"Okaaay", he replied. "So we are going to visit Surt's sister, the mother of all frost-giants, a being every bit as powerful and frightening as Surt, and you don't think we need to make preparations. Please tell me why."

Now Snorri swung his left leg over Galdrafaxi's hindquarters and dismounted. He faced Shiner, who was a full head taller than him, but he now felt equal in stature.

"I have figured it out", he said, simply. "It's all illusion, isn't it? Everything that we have so far encountered has been illusion, presented in such a way that I could digest the lessons. Do the Vanir really live in a simple, wooden hall and spend their days gardening? Do the Light-Elves live in a castle in the clouds? Does Surt really take the form of a man, however fiery and gigantic? Do Dwarfs really have long beards?"

He looked up at the constantly shifting aurora, and took a deep breath of the icy air.

"May I have another draught of that mead?", he asked. "It helps me to think more clearly."

Shiner nodded, and handed him the flask. Snorri took a gulp, wiped his lips, and handed it back.

"It started to come to me after you told me to get dressed by imagining it, and I put on the finest clothes that I could picture, to make an impression. Not that Surt cared much!"

He laughed, and continued.

"And then you explained about the avatars; how Gods change their appearance to match our level of understanding. That clinched it really. It's all about telling a story. Tell a story in the right way, and it becomes reality for those listening. Tell it with enough conviction, and it becomes reality for the teller. And I am a master story-teller. Cold here, isn't it?"

He clicked his fingers, and a fire sprang into existence on the road. Shiner could feel the heat radiating from it, and Galdrafaxi snorted and moved towards it.

"This I understand: it is going to be cold where we are going" (Shiner was startled to see that Snorri was now wearing a thick, fur coat with matching boots and trousers) "so the main thing is that you should tell me all about Niflheim, about Jökulheið, and everything we are likely to experience. "
And with that, he sat close to the fire and warmed his hands.

At first, Shiner had no idea what to say. Initially, he had taken Snorri to be a small, impressionable mortal – no, only the ghost of a mortal – whose education had been assigned to him for reasons unknown. He had already discerned that Snorri was a fast learner, quick of wit, and stubbornly resolute, but this development was simply extraordinary. Snorri was fast becoming his equal. Could it be that his own knowledge had seeped into Snorri by osmosis? He deemed it unlikely. Perhaps Snorri was simply a prodigy. Whatever the case, the fire was welcoming, a manifestation worthy of his own skill, and he sat down by Snorri, warmed his hands, and took a swig of the mead himself.
"Snorri Sturluson", he said, "you are a remarkable creature. Never before have I seen anyone grasp the mysteries with such alacrity."
Snorri rubbed his hands together close to the flames.
"Oh, I don't know", he smiled, "it's taken at least four hundred years. You said so yourself."

Shiner stared into the fire, wondering how long Snorri could make it last. He was tempted to just sit there and find out, but there was still a mission to be accomplished and Midgard's effect could still be felt. Time was a factor.
"We have to get on", he said, "but you are right: we need not go about it the way that I would have done customarily. I say 'customarily', but I have to admit that I am simply making it up as I go, using my skills to improvise. As you also have some skill, and wisdom, let us approach this as allies."
"Then tell me what you know", replied Snorri.
"That would take a very long time, my friend" Shiner said, "but I will tell you the things that are relevant to the task ahead."

He made a pass of his hand, and was suddenly also clad in warm furs. Galdrafaxi gave a satisfied whinny and shook himself as a thick caparison appeared, covering him all the way down to his knees. "The destinations that we covered first were the easiest", Shiner continued. "It is always a bit of a problem for the living to enter Hel, whence I retrieved you, but I had done it before. Garm, the Hel-hound, is a soft old thing once he gets to know you, and I brought him some of his favourite treats. After that, we visited worlds with which I am thoroughly acquainted, and where I am welcome to varying extents. You saw how well received we were in the homes of the Dark Elves and the Vanir; those people I count as friends. Even those obsequious prats, the Light Elves, put on a show for us. As you gathered, I don't like them very much with all their lofty pretensions, but they have a function, as do all the denizens of the Nine Worlds. Once we get to Asgard, the Boss himself will take over, and it will be out of my hands for a while. Perhaps he will tell you the purpose of this entire mission, and I hope that I am allowed to stick around and hear it too. After that, we go to Etin-home. I know the Etins well enough to say that you have nothing to fear from them, though they may revel in deluding you. What happens after that, I don't know."

Snorri nodded, identifying the omissions, and Shiner went on. "Why the Boss insisted that you were to visit Muspelsheim and Niflheim also, I do not know. I had never seen them, except at a distance, and all that I knew was that they were inhabited by beings far older than the Gods and the Etins: dangerous, unknowable beings who were extremely hazardous to approach and unlikely to impart any information. I feared for our existence – mine as well as yours – and said as much, but he was insistent. He said he was confident that I would muddle through somehow. And muddle through I did. My magic gave us protection long enough to allow us to talk to Surt. Like you, I had thought that Surt was implacably hostile to men and Gods, that he would never give us a hearing and would try to burn our souls away. That was why I took such elaborate precautions and, even then, I had little faith that they would be enough. Believe me, Snorri, I learned as much as you did from that encounter: there is no implacable hostility; we will simply get in the way when two lovers meet again, aeons from now. I doubt whether the Boss knows that... I guess I shall have to tell him."

Snorri nodded again, glad of this unaccustomed candour.

"So that just leaves us with Niflheim and its icy Queen", he said. "What do you know of her?"

Shiner puffed his cheeks and opened his eyes wide.

"Not much. Legends say that she is the polar opposite of Surt. He is all heat and bright, expansive energy. She is as cold as cold gets, but attractive. In the literal sense. She will draw us in, deeper and deeper, compressing our beings and burying them under ice. Unable to escape. Ever. All this I discussed with the Dwarfs, while you were being shown their work, and with the Vanir while you slept in their hall. They advised me to avoid this part of the quest, to make something up to tell the Boss. But that is not possible; he always detects a lie. Again I must muddle through, but now I have someone to help me with that. Don't I?"

"Yes, you have", Snorri replied. He held out his hand, and Shiner accepted it and shook it.

"What do know you of the runes?", Shiner asked.

"Do you mean 'runes' as mysteries, or as script?", Snorri answered. "I know little of mysteries, but I know all sixteen tokens of the row, from *Fé* to *Yr*. And I can remember some of the little verses associated with them. We don't use them so much now – or rather, we didn't when I was alive – because the Roman letters are easier to write with pen and parchment, and there are more of them, so you have more choice."

"Well, that's a very good start", said Shiner. "Those tokens embody some of the mysteries, for those who can be bothered to learn them, and the little verses that you mentioned are keys to those mysteries. There is no time now to teach you all about this, but know that I use their power a lot in the magic that I work. For example, I made great use of the sign *Ís* – Ice – in preparation for our visit to Surt. It kept us cool in the face of the heat. Now we have to make use of other runes to protect us against the cold."

He reached inside his coat, drew out a rolled parchment, and spread it. The fire's light had begun to fade, making it difficult to read by, so Shiner passed the parchment over the flames. The runic characters shone, clearly visible on the page, and Shiner's finger pointed to the ones he had chosen.

"To defend us against the cold, I am minded to use this one, *Ken*, which means 'torch', and this one, *Nyd*, which we can use to kindle fire, then *Sigel* – Sun, always the enemy of Ice – and *Daeg* – Day – for shining light in that dark realm. Does that make sense to you?"

Snorri was confused. He recognised the characters that meant 'Need' and 'Sun', but not the other two. He counted the characters in the row, and came to twenty-eight.

"What runes are these?", he asked. "There are so many that I do not know."

Shiner realised his error and the source of Snorri's confusion.

"Ah...", he said, "I am sorry, these are English runes. As with your Roman letters, there are more of them, so one has more choice. 'Need' and 'Sun' you will undoubtedly recognise. *Ken* is the equivalent of your *Kaun*, and..."

Snorri interrupted him.

"Wait a minute", he interjected, "I remember the poem for that rune. It's all about sores and ulcers, baleful for children. How will that help us?"

"Well observed", Shiner replied, "and it is good that you ask, for we must be of one mind when we work together with these signs. In the old lore, hundreds of years before your time, the concepts of 'torch' and 'sore' were combined. The old poem ran something along the lines of

'Torch burns brightly in the hall,
Its light a boon to all;
But the unwitting child who grasps it
May be burned sorely.'

"As always, fire is useful but also dangerous to those do not handle it carefully. Unfortunately, these aspects became divorced in the

English poem and the one that you are familiar with. Does that make sense?"

Snorri nodded, and looked at the parchment again. The light in the characters was moving, dynamic. In the one Shiner had called 'Day', a particularly bright point moved up a vertical stroke, then down a diagonal stroke, up the opposing vertical stroke, and then down the other diagonal to the point where it had started. He found it an entrancing sight, and asked what it meant. Again, Shiner was happy to explain.

"It is called 'Day', but it embodies the whole idea of a day, which, of course, is made up of the dark hours and the bright hours. The node in the centre represents dusk and dawn, when it is neither night nor day, a time that is ever at the edge. It is a paradox, for it is neither one thing or the other, yet both at the same time. However, I intend to use only its bright aspect to light our way."

Snorri considered this, tracing with his finger the course of the light along the rune.

"So it is a rune of transformation, one thing constantly turning into its opposite?"

Shiner was used by now to Snorri's quick wit, but at this he was genuinely astonished.

"By the Gods!", he exclaimed, "You are a quick learner. You might make an excellent Rune-master, and it is only a pity that I do not have the leisure to teach you fully."

But Snorri had not yet finished.

"We can use that", he said. "It means we can transform cold into its opposite, into heat. And we can even remain comfortable, if we focus on the node where there is neither cold nor heat."

Shiner threw up his arms and raised his eyes to the blackness above them in joy. Then he stood and brushed frost from the back of his fur jacket where the fire's warmth had not reached, laughing in delight.

"Then there is nothing left to work out! Let us get on with it. Your contribution will be invaluable."

By the light of the fading fire, they performed a ritual similar to the one that Shiner had used before the encounter with Surt, but now Snorri was a full partner in the working. They used different runes, runes of heat, light, and transformation. At the closing of the rite, their skins and clothes glowed with these runes, and Galdrafaxi was likewise bedecked. Shiner had created a talisman, which he wore on a thong around his neck, and from it an orb of warm orange radiated around the travellers. They felt confident. The last flames of the fire that Snorri had kindled flickered into nothingness as he climbed up behind Shiner's saddle, and they set off, resuming their northward journey.

"Only a pity that we may not use that ember from Muspelsheim", said Shiner, turning slightly. "It might make a difference, but I respect your wish."
Snorri patted the shoulder of his guide; his guide who had become his friend.
"Oh, I think it will make a difference", he replied. "In fact, I think it will be our trump card."

It steadily became yet colder, and the road terminated at a shore of black, gritty sand. Under a leaden sky, ice floes and bergs rode on the sea as the waves lapped sullenly against the strand. There was no sound, apart from the lapping of the waves; no cry of gull pierced the air, and even the air was still and windless. A half-light prevailed, though whether of dawn or dusk Snorri could not tell. It struck him that it might always be thus in this miserable, lifeless place.
"This is it", Shiner announced, "we are at the border of Niflheim."
With narrowed eyes, Snorri surveyed the scene, which was one of utter bleakness, the negation of life and hope. Even Hel had been comfortable compared to this, a place of quiet rest that offered the prospect of rebirth. This was the antithesis of his fiery, Christian Hell: a place of numbing cold and loneliness, without even the companionship of other tormented souls.

"It has to be an illusion", he muttered under his breath. "It is painted too perfectly, as if to match my expectations."

He started to open his mind, willing the illusion away with the aim of seeing what lay beneath. The desolate surroundings began to quiver, and outlines became less distinct.

"STOP!", immediately shouted Shiner, who had somewhat read his mind. "Please accept the metaphor, the allegory. You were right: it is all illusion. Dwarfs do not have long beards, nor has Surt the shape of a man. But these appearances are put up to defend you from the bare reality, which would deprive you of your mind. Accept them, for your sanity's sake!"

Snorri accepted Shiner's advice, and ceased his attempt to penetrate the illusion. The strand, the sea and the ice floes came back into focus, bleak and barren as they had been before. If the bare reality was worse than this, he thought, it must be terrible indeed.

"As you will realise", said Shiner, "we can go no further on horseback. We must cross this dreadful sea by boat, and Galdrafaxi must wait for our return."

They dismounted, and Shiner unbuckled one of the saddle bags, slinging it over one shoulder. He whispered some words into Galdrafaxi's ear, and the horse turned and sped away, back along the path by which they had come. With Shiner leading, they trudged the sodden shoreline until they came upon a small, black boat that was just big enough for the two of them. Within its hull were two paddles, and a long pole projected over the gunwales. Shiner dumped the saddle bag into the boat and asked Snorri to help him launch the boat into the water. Together, they pushed it over the grating sand, then leaped in once it was afloat. Shiner took the pole and propelled the boat out across the shallows. Snorri, in the prow, looked back, and thought that Shiner, with his long cloak and hood, looked every inch the image of Charon in the mythology of the Greeks. After only a few strokes, the depth increased so that the pole was useless, so Shiner laid it inside the hull, sat on a thwart, and took up a paddle. Snorri also took up a paddle, and together they wove a path between the treacherous ice floes and

bergs towards the opposite shore. A wind rose, and snow began to fall from the grey clouds overhead, but to their relief it sizzled, melted, and ran from the glowing, orange sphere that surrounded them. The sphere also helped to enhance their progress, melting away the ice when it lay in a thin skim upon the sea's surface, but eventually thick ice completely barred their way and they could paddle no further. Stepping onto a stationary floe, they hauled the light skiff from the water and dragged it landward for many yards across the rocking ice until they found a sound and stable surface. It was still sea-ice, but it did not appear likely to be going anywhere for the foreseeable future. Panting after the effort, Shiner spoke.
"That's the best we can do. From here on, we walk."
Snorri nodded and cast his eyes about the landscape, taking mental bearings on snow-crowned peaks in the hope that they might have a chance of finding the skiff again when they returned. *If they returned*. The thought entered his mind, but he dismissed it instantly. He had to be positive. He must write this story as if it had already happened; that was their only source of salvation in this grand illusion. Looking at the scene that surrounded them, a colourless desolation of white and grey, he raised his voice and spoke aloud.
"We came. We fulfilled our mission. We came away unscathed."
Shiner had been slinging the saddlebag over his shoulder again, and looked up.
"What was that?", he asked.
"Just some magic", Snorri replied, "I'm getting the hang of it, as I said. It's all about the narrative."
Shiner grunted in reply and stepped up to lead again, Snorri noting that he looked tired. He had blue smudges below his eyes, and the end of his nose was white and bloodless. The cold outside the orb must be truly fierce, Snorri thought, and was thankful for the talisman that glowed warmly even through the furs that Shiner wore. Pushing through knee-deep snow, they forged onward into the heart of Niflheim, the wind growing in force and the snow flurries becoming thicker and more frequent, until they were in the midst of a howling blizzard. It was impossible to see beyond the

perimeter of the orange sphere. Though the blizzard did not pierce the orb, it became cold enough for snow to form inside it and for frost to form. Icicles hung from their beards and eyebrows. Outside the sphere, the snow accumulated rapidly. They halted, totally uncertain of which direction to take.

"What now?", Snorri shouted above the roar of the gale.

Shiner did not answer, but went down on one knee and dropped the saddle bag onto the snow before him. He removed his mittens and, with shaking hands, undid a buckle. The leather was stiff and resistant, and Snorri saw the pained expression on Shiner's face as his bare flesh touched the freezing metal of the buckle. Shiner reached an arm into the bag, groped blindly for a moment or two, then brought out another talisman and hung it about Snorri's neck. Snorri inspected the emblem that it bore: a radial glyph consisting of eight spokes, each spoke terminating in a different combination of forks and curves.

"It is called *Vegvísir*, the signpost", said Shiner. He gave a racking cough. "With that stave, we can find our way, even in a storm, in unfamiliar territory." He coughed again. "Would you mind taking the lead?", he asked, "I am... a little tired, and it is hard work pressing through this snow."

Snorri fingered the talisman and looked around them at the racing flakes that flew horizontally on the raging gale.

"How will I know?", he asked, "How do I use it?"

Shiner staggered to his feet, slinging the saddle bag over his shoulder again.

"Just put one foot in front of the other", he replied, "the *Vegvísir* will show you the way. Trust in it."

Snorri did as he was bidden and pushed on through thigh-deep snow, using his mittened hands as well to dig a path. The twilight had given way to complete darkness and the only light came from the glow of the orb. He felt the need for more light, and remembered the rune that Shiner had taught him. "*Ken!*", he uttered, and a burning brand appeared in the air before him. He grasped its shaft, and it felt solid enough, but the light did little more than illuminate the flying snowflakes better. Disappointed, he pushed on, listening to Shiner's racking cough behind him. Whenever that sound became more distant, he slowed and gave his friend time to catch up. They took frequent rest breaks, and the intervals between the breaks became shorter and shorter. Eventually, at one such break, Shiner collapsed to lie prostrate on the snow. His breathing was shallow and laboured, except when he gave those terrible coughs that seemed to tear him part. *Huuurgh! Huurgh!* Now Snorri was genuinely concerned. He kneeled beside the prostrate Shiner, removed his mittens and his own, and tried to rub warmth into the frozen hands.

"Tell me what to do", he pleaded, "is there no magic left? What about the other runes, the runes of kindling, and sun, and transformation? Can we not call upon them now?"

Shiner blinked hard a time or two, opening his eyes wide between each blink. His panting breaths were short and rapid.

"We used it all", he gasped. "It all went into the making of the talisman, and I fear we may have been over-optimistic."

Snorri pulled the *Vegvísir* from beneath his furs and fingered it.

"No, not that one", Shiner said weakly. "The one that I wear, the one that shines this lovely, orange globe around us. Outside, it is as cold as cold can be. Without it, we would already be dead. Be thankful for small mercies."

Snorri sat on the snow, wondering what to do. He looked at the saddle bag. Might there be something in there that he could use, even to get Shiner back to the shore and across the icy sea? It seemed that their mission had failed, so he might as well at least try to save his companion. Shiner appeared to have fallen asleep and Snorri was shivering uncontrollably, feeling overcome by despair. In desperation, he looked at his own pouch and opened it, to be met by a bright light. Out of it he fished the bracket fungus and its ember, except that the ember was now emitting an intense light and, even more welcome, heat, though it had not consumed the fungus or burned the pouch. He took it and warmed his own hands, then passed it slowly over Shiner's body from toes to head. Shiner began to stir and moan, finally sitting up and wiping the frozen snot from his nose.

"Why did you wake me?", he exclaimed. "I was having a beautiful dream, in which I met my perfect lover."
Snorri breathed a sigh of relief.
"I think you were dying", he answered, "but thanks to Surt's fire you were saved. Can you get up? We need to get out of here and return to safer climes. Our mission is accomplished, I think. I have seen Niflheim, and I will leave the ember here for its Queen to find, so I have kept my pledge to Surt. More cannot be asked of us, surely?"
Shiner was scrambling to his feet. He staggered and stumbled, and was still beset by the dreadful cough, but a feverish light of determination shone in his eyes.
"No!", he cried, "I have seen her now, and we must go on! It cannot be far."
His knees wobbled as he picked up the saddle bag, checked that the buckle was secure, and cast it over his shoulder.
"Are you serious?", Snorri asked, amazed. "You were nearly dead. You warned me that this might be our most dangerous undertaking, and so it has proved. I'll leave the gift for Jökulheið to find, and we can return. To warmth. To safety."
But Shiner only mumbled something in reply as he staggered deeper into the interior, bent under the weight of the bag.
"Why don't you let me carry that?", Snorri suggested, "or ditch the damned thing altogether. It only burdens you. If we have not far to go, as you say, then we shall not have need of it. It is only so much dead weight now."
Shiner trudged forward through the snow as the blizzard continued to rage. Between coughs, he shouted back to Snorri.
"It contains my heart and body. Please don't ask. And I know the way now. Just follow!"

# Chapter 9 - Jökulheið

Together they forced their way through the mounting snow drifts, Snorri following along the path trampled by Shiner, the latter's previous exhaustion now overcome by a fanaticism. Heading between the heights, they entered a gorge, and here the wind dropped and became still. The snow, too, ceased falling, but the cold increased in intensity, penetrating to the marrow. The glowing, orange sphere that had protected them began to flicker as the sky cleared and stars appeared overhead. They were enveloped in an atmosphere of icy, deadly calm, and then they heard the singing of a beautiful, female voice. It sang a promise of rest and pleasure. Snorri was entranced. Drawing on final reserves of energy, Shiner rushed forward along a stony path that was miraculously unimpeded.

"Come on, Snorri!", Shiner shouted with joy, "can you not hear her? She calls us. She calls me to be her lover!"

Without trepidation, Snorri hastened behind Shiner, anxious not to lose the protection of the orange sphere, tenuous though it now appeared. A light, a bluish-white light, came into view ahead of them at the other end of the gill, and as they approached it resolved itself into the shape of a female figure. She was clad in a voluminous coat of white cloth, trimmed with fur and blue embroidery, and her head was surmounted by a tall, fur-trimmed hat decorated with lace, into which snowflake patterns were woven. From under the hat, flaxen braids fell to her shoulders, and between the descending tresses was the most beautiful face that one could imagine, with shining, blue eyes, high cheek-bones and ruby-red lips. She reminded Snorri of tales told to him by the Swedish Rus, of the snow-maiden revered by the Slavs they ruled in Novgorod, the daughter of Father Frost. She smiled, an innocent and welcoming smile.

"Come to me", she said.

Snorri was overcome with desire. Here, at last, was an end to all their travel and suffering. Shiner even more so; he began to cast off his protective clothing, shouting "I come to you, my love!"

Enamoured, they both kneeled before the vision that seemed the sum of all their desires.

Staring, unable to shift his gaze, Snorri fumbled in his pouch and again withdrew the ember. He held it out, cupped in the palms of his hands, to the ice-maiden, and now it shone like a beacon. "Jökulheið", he said in an awe-struck tone, "glad we are to meet you. We have travelled far, and I bring you a gift, a token, from Surt, your lover. Please accept it."
The face grew suddenly hard. The smile disappeared and the tenderness in the eyes was replaced by a tight frown of anger.
"WHO DARES TO SPEAK MY TRUE NAME?", bellowed the shining apparition. A black hole appeared in her bosom, at first only a point, but expanding rapidly until the gorgeous snow-maiden was entirely blotted out. The voice spoke again, and it was the deep, resonating grinding of glaciers, the calving of icebergs, and the howling of the storm.
"I ASK AGAIN. WHO ARE YOU, AND WHO GAVE YOU MY TRUE NAME? SPEAK, BEFORE YOU DIE!"
Snorri's fright propelled him back onto his behind, and he scrabbled backwards in the thin snow that covered the rocks. The black hole continued to expand until it formed the pupil of a gigantic eye that threatened to envelop him and everything he knew. He still clutched the piece of bracket fungus in his clenched fist. Its light was now blinding, but it seemed to send out a thought.
"I did not promise you that this would be easy, man-ghost", it said. "My sister-lover is as terrible as I am; perhaps more so. Just hand it over, and I will see that all ends well."
Still terrified, Snorri forced himself to his knees again, drew his arm back, and hurled the flaming parcel into the centre of the eye. It swirled and spiralled, sending out a shower of sparks, then was lost and consumed in the blackness of the eye. Then there was only silence, for how long Snorri could not say. It was followed by a sob that rippled through the nine worlds. In the tiny part of Midgard that men call Earth, glaciers extended, crops failed, there was widespread starvation, and frost fairs were held on the frozen River

Thames. But in Niflheim, at least, all was still. With the gigantic eye still before him, Snorri felt his arms, legs and torso. All pretty solid, he thought... well, as solid as he had ever been since he died and Shiner retrieved him from Hel. Shiner... he looked to his left at his friend, who kneeled still with a rapturous smile on his face, and reached over to tug at his shoulder.
"Shiner!", he gasped, grinning. "Shiner! Hey, I think we pulled it off. We're still alive! Well, I am... sort of. Come on, job done. Let's get out of here."
Shiner remained motionless, and Snorri registered the frozen glaze on the eyes, the blue lips, and the absence of breath issuing from those lips. Horrified, he released his grip of the shoulder and gave a slight push. Shiner fell sideways, frozen and stiff. He was dead.

For a long time, Snorri squatted before the unblinking eye, staring at Shiner's corpse, dismayed. It didn't make sense. Why had Shiner died, while he had not? He tried hard to unravel his thoughts.
"Wait a minute, he thought, I'm already dead; how much more dead can I be? Shiner and the dwarfs said that I was more solid than I should ever be. How can this still be so, in this realm that is so inimical to all existence?"
He reviewed all the events that had preceded this disastrous encounter. He had first donned a torc that held him together, and after that had drunk an awful lot of magical mead with the Dark Elves, red wine with the Vanir and some airy kind of wine with the Light Elves. Then he had had a meeting with a primal fire-giant, who had given him a package to deliver; surely some power must have come of all that? The message from the ember had said that deliverance was at hand. He was still dead; of that, there could be no doubt, but he could still think and hold all of his memories. He felt cold, which meant that he retained the memory of being cold. Somewhere... sometime... long ago. And for some reason Jökulheið, Queen of Niflheim, had not stolen his soul. The unblinking eye was still watching him as he turned back to Shiner's rigid body. The physical body lay where it had fallen, but the ghost remained kneeling and appeared to be dissolving, steadily becoming thinner

and more transparent. It reminded him of his experiences in Svartálfheim, the home of those kindly and industrious Dwarfs, his first encounter after he had been woken in Hel. He examined Shiner's increasingly tenuous ghostly head, and found he could see inside it. An idea, a hope, came to him. Opening the discarded saddle bag, he rummaged within it and brought out two empty glass bottles, a long tweezer, and a bodkin. He took the tweezer and, as gently as he could, extracted the hard, angular gem that he recognised as Shiner's cognition. Forcing his hand to be steady, he guided it into the first bottle and then stoppered it tightly with its cork. The next task was more delicate, but he remembered the procedure adopted by the Dwarfs. Delicately inserting the bodkin into the fading apparition of Shiner's head, he identified the skein of memories and wound it around the tip. When he was sure that all the memories were on the tip and unbroken, he painstakingly inserted it into the second bottle and teased them free, then stoppered this bottle also. So far, so good, he thought, but what of Shiner's soul? He assumed that it must have been drawn in by Jökulheið, forever to rest, compressed and impotent, in frozen stillness. The black pupil of the unblinking eye still regarded him: impassive, uncaring, yet curious; and he decided on a final gamble. He owed it to Shiner. He stood and faced the blackness, pulled his shoulders back, and made his boast.

"Great Jökulheið! Essence of Ice and mother of Thurses! I stand before you – I – Snorri Sturluson, far-traveller, Dwarf-friend, Vana-friend, guest of Elves, escaped from Hel and beloved of Surt. I journeyed far between Muspelsheim and Niflheim with but one thought in mind: to bring you a spark, a token of love from your fiery husband. You are mighty and I am small, so I have little to lose. Will it be said that the Queen of Niflheim denied a small boon to a poor messenger who carried a precious parcel so far?"

There was a long silence in which Snorri stared into utter blackness. Then that voice came again, the grinding of glaciers.

"WHAT BOON DO YOU CRAVE?"

Again, Snorri puffed himself up. He felt so ridiculous, challenging a primaeval force, but he forced himself to go on.

"All I want", he said, "is the soul of the one I know as Shiner, the being who came here with me. You sucked it in, and I know you have it. Give it to me, for Surt's sake, else I shall return to him and tell him that the gift was not well received, and that you slew the guide of the bearer."

There followed a pause, a pause so long that Snorri began to fear that his demand had not been heard. The black pupil still stood before him, but at length he felt a lessening of its devouring force. Then, astonishingly, Jökulheið blinked. And she laughed as well, a long, low chuckle that sounded like the roar of an avalanche.

"I LIKE YOU, SNORRI, SON OF STURLA", she said, "YOU HAVE BALLS. ARE YOU SURE YOU DO NOT WISH TO COME TO ME?"

For a moment the gigantic eye disappeared, to be replaced by the previous vision of the most desirable woman Snorri might imagine. The snow-maiden's arms were spread enticingly, her head inclined slightly to one side, and a coquettish smile wreathed her lips. Her face was a mask of invitation, tenderness and promise. The biting cold was replaced by an impression of pleasurable warmth and, despite the absence of a mortal body, Snorri felt his *hamr* experience the ghost of an erection. The temptation was almost overwhelming, but he remembered that the same desire had led Shiner to his death and, head bowed, he forced himself to see beyond the illusion. The vision vanished and the eye and the cold returned.

"Thank you, Qu... Queen of Niflheim", he stammered. "But all I crave is the soul of my friend."

Jökulheið sighed, the moan of an Arctic wind.

"A PITY", she said, "YOU MIGHT HAVE AMUSED ME FOR A WHILE, FOR YOU ARE A STRONG ONE. YOU MENTIONED A SOUL; WHICH ONE WAS IT AGAIN? I HAVE SO MANY. SOME CALL MY REALM NIFLHEL. HEL SENDS ME THE SOULS THAT SHE REJECTS – THE SINNERS, THE DEFILERS, THE INCORRIGIBLE. THOSE WHO ARE NEVER TO BE BORN AGAIN. I HAVE A SACKFUL OF THEM."

Snorri forced himself to be patient and diplomatic, having no other choice.

"My Lady", he replied, "having seen your power – and that of your inestimable husband, Surt of Muspelsheim – I cannot imagine that your great intelligence would fail to remember each individual soul. This one was but a recent acquisition, and he was not a sinner as far as I am aware. He came here with me, and his name was Shiner. Please give him to me."

There was no spoken response, but from the centre of the vast eye a small light floated, no brighter than a firefly or a distant candle at first. It grew in intensity as it approached and, when it was within arm's reach, Snorri grasped it gently, guided it into a third bottle and then replaced the cork. He bowed and uttered his thanks, then shouldered the bag, turned and walked away without a backward glance, relieved that the encounter was finally over. For many minutes, he could feel the eye's gaze on the nape of his neck, then the sensation ceased and he was utterly alone.

Using the *Vegvísir* talisman to guide his steps, Snorri trudged and waded back through the snow to where the skiff lay beached, using the runes that he had learned to light the way and dispel the cold. Eventually, he stood beside the boat and dumped the saddle bag into it. He turned around to look at the towering peaks, feeling numb of heart as well as from the cold. How was it possible that Shiner, his friend and guide, was dead? How had he, Snorri, survived the same ordeal? He felt guilty for failing his friend, even though logic dictated that he could have done no more. The misery sat like a baleful lump in his chest as he punted the skiff into the water and began to paddle towards the opposite shore. Perhaps, he thought, Shiner had come to adorn himself with the comfortable accoutrements of mortality, and had thereby acquired the concomitant weaknesses and vulnerabilities. Had he, Snorri, so recently alive, been responsible for this? He hated to think it, but he could not dismiss the idea. Shiner had been so hard, decisive and disdainful when they had first met, but he had warmed to him, Snorri, since the meeting with Surt. Paddling across the ice-girt sea, Snorri could only imagine that Shiner had been fatally weakened by all his efforts and by empathy with a mortal but recently deceased, and the responsibility weighed heavy on his shoulders.

After a seemingly endless amount of paddling, the boat's prow at last slid into the sodden, black sand. Again the air was still, and the grey half-light prevailed; it was a shore of deadness and despair. Snorri dragged the skiff a little higher until it was fully out of the water, then unloaded the saddle bag that had been so precious to Shiner. He squelched across the liminal space between sea and land until he found himself above the tide-line, then collapsed, with his bottom on the black, gritty sand. He felt exhausted, though more by emotion than any physical effort. His tears created runnels through the black dirt that clothed his face, and he sobbed until all emotion was dispelled and only rationality remained. Head down, clutching his knees, he heard the voice of his grandmother. "Well, this'll not do. Better make a start." Encouraged by the memory, he stood and tried to summon Galdrafaxi. He shouted the horse's name and whistled for all he was worth, but there was no answering whinny or thump of hoofs. That was a blow; his plan had been to ride Galdrafaxi to Asgard - the horse would surely know the way - where Odin would possess the magic to bring Shiner back to life. Disappointed, Snorri found a boulder to sit on while he reviewed his options. Staying on this miserable, unchanging shore was definitely not an option. Quite apart from the soul-destroying wretchedness of the surroundings, he knew that he would lose energy and disintegrate before long; only the company of Gods, Elves and Dwarfs, plus copious draughts of Shiner's life-giving elixir had allowed him so far to maintain a form that was nearly as solid as any living human. Without these, he would eventually become a lost and gibbering wraith, forever to haunt this place of dread. Nor was leaving an option, without assistance from Shiner and Galdrafaxi, for – despite his earlier threat to return to Muspelsheim – he knew not the way to any of the other worlds. He picked up the saddle bag again and, on an impulse, emptied its contents onto the sand. What was it that Shiner had said about it containing his body? Rifling among the various items, Snorri found a rune-inscribed knife, the wand with which Shiner had once threatened him (it seemed so long ago, and probably was), a hide-bound book of spells, and a flagon containing about an inch of the life-giving elixir. There were also two leather sacks, one larger than the other. Opening the larger one, he found that it contained bone ash; he recognised it well, for during his lifetime there had still been heathens who cremated their dead instead of burying them. The smaller sack contained what at first appeared to be a dry and shrivelled piece of meat but, on closer examination of the large, arterial apertures, revealed itself to be a mummified human heart. Doubtless, these must have been what Shiner had referred to as his body, though Snorri could not imagine the magic or motives involved in all of this. Nevertheless, the germ of an idea came to him. If he could not reach Odin to revivify Shiner, then perhaps he might attempt the deed himself? After all, he had Shiner's heart and ashes, and in the three glass vials were his soul, thought and memories, retrieved from Niflheim. Excitedly, he picked up the book of spells and flicked through the vellum pages until he found what he was looking for. Before him was a page that bore the title *Til að vekja upp draug* – to awaken a *draugr*. Snorri shuddered, and not because of the cold. He was entirely familiar with the concept. A *draugr* was a reanimated corpse, raised by the actions of a sorcerer, usually for malign purposes. He remembered folk tales that said you didn't even need the whole corpse – one or two bones were all that were necessary. A complex stave was depicted on the page, and the accompanying text gave precise instructions. True, these called for the use of some ingredients that Snorri neither had, nor had any hope of obtaining, such as the blood of a raven and of a seal, but he felt confident that he could make substitutions. He had the key elements of Shiner's body. More importantly, he had his soul, thought and memories, which meant that Shiner would not merely be a shambling, mindless being. It had to be worth the attempt; indeed, it was the only course of action available.

Still sitting on the boulder, Snorri took a swig of the remaining elixir and kindled a fire in the manner that had so surprised Shiner. Then he cleared his mind and forced himself to be confident, for he had noticed that many of the spells concluded with an injunction to 'have great faith'. He focused on all his memories of Shiner: his knowledge, his wry humour, his arrogance, but also his compassion and occasional vulnerability. When he had the most perfect mental image that he could muster, Snorri carefully scattered the ash on the ground in the shape of a man, the whitish ash standing out starkly against the black sand. Then he placed the shrivelled heart in the correct place, and deposited the contents of the three bottles – soul, mind and memory - on the crown of the head. In the utterly still air, he had no worry that these fragile elements might be blown away. Next, he traced the magical stave in the sand above the head, meticulously copying it from the book, and sprinkled what was left of the elixir onto the torso area. He had no blood to give, but he used the magical knife anyway to score his own left forearm and was satisfied to see a thin stream of ectoplasm flow onto the ashen image. Standing again, Snorri began the rite prescribed in the book. He hailed the wights of the four points of the compass, simply guessing where those might be, and called upon all the Gods to witness his intent and give assistance. He was tempted to include Jehovah, Christ and the Virgin Mary, but decided they probably would not have approved. Having completed the opening words and gestures, he began the incantation, reciting it over and over until the words lost any meaning for his conscious mind. As he chanted, he fell into a trance and unfamiliar, barbaric words began to interject themselves until his voice rose and fell in a steady ululation that was in no language known to man. How long he continued this, he could not say, as there was no way of gauging time in this grey environment of everlasting dusk, but eventually exhaustion overcame him and he fell to the sand on his right side, facing the object of his sorcery. Nothing had changed. The ash lay there as before, and Shiner had not reappeared. His energy almost totally depleted, his only gambit unsuccessful, Snorri closed his eyes, too tired to care anymore. He had failed.

Snorri dreamed a confusing, frightening dream. It had begun well enough as an erotic fantasy, in which he was about to mate with the Snow Maiden. She had spread her legs for him but, as he was about to enter her, her vagina expanded wider and wider until it was a gaping, black hole into which he tumbled headlong. He fell for a long time before he saw a small light in the distance, which turned out to be a candle shining weakly on a table. At the table sat Shiner, reading his book of magic spells. Without looking up, he told Snorri not to worry: he was working on a new spell that would have them out of there in... oh, a couple of thousand years. Then a party of Dwarfs entered. Their leader said "Time for you to be dismantled, Mister Snorri. Now you just hold still, and we'll have your thoughts and memories out of you in a jiffy." He protested, but the Dwarfs pinned him to the floor, holding his head fast as the long tweezer approached his cranium. Odin appeared and stood over him, laughing, and prodded his side with *Gungnir*, his spear. Snorri tried in vain to move, becoming frantic with anxiety. He could neither speak nor move a muscle until he mustered his last resources and let out a desperate scream... and awoke.

Shiner was standing over him, prodding Snorri's ribs with his toe. Snorri sat bolt upright, wildly looking all around him and wondering whether he was still dreaming. The fire still burned, feebly now, but still emitting some heat, and the sea still lapped on the endless black shoreline. He rubbed his eyes, and Shiner still stood next to him, naked and smiling. Snorri tentatively reached out and touched a foot; it was warm, except where the sole met the sand, and there it was icy cold. In a flurry of movement, he got to his feet and looked over Shiner from the smiling face to the cold feet, and back again. Shiner said simply "Where are my clothes?"
Snorri babbled.
"We have to get you dressed before you freeze to death! Your clothes... yes, your clothes... just use your imagination... you know how to do that!"
Shiner stared at his own limbs, seeming dazed.
"I... I can't remember how to do it", he said.

"Then let me try", Snorri answered, and he called forth his imagination and visualisation to dress Shiner in warm, sealskin boots, mittens, trousers and jacket, with the fur facing to the inside. Shiner surveyed his new garb with a bemused smile, stamped his feet and flexed his arms.
"That's impressive", he said. "Who taught you that?"
"Why, you did!", Snorri replied.
"Did I?", said Shiner. "Then it must have been a long time ago, for I cannot remember it."
Snorri looked carefully at the face. It was the same as before: the same aquiline nose and chiselled features, the same dark-brown, shoulder-length hair. Only the eyes were different; they were guileless and vacant, the eyes of an idiot or a new-born infant. Taking Shiner gently by the arm, he guided him to the boulder, sat him down, and squatted before him.
"What is the last thing that you remember?", he asked.
Shiner looked all around him for several seconds, the imbecile smile still on his lips.
"I remember a beautiful woman. It was really cold, but she was warm. I wanted to go to her. After that... just blackness. And then I woke up here. What is this place? It looks pretty awful." He giggled.
Snorri patted the backs of Shiner's mittened hands and stared earnestly into the vacant eyes.
"Listen carefully, Shiner. We are in great danger here. It doesn't matter for now how we came here, or why, but we must leave. Now. Can you remember your horse, Galdrafaxi? Can you summon him?"
To Snorri's relief, that memory appeared to be intact, and a spark of the old Shiner was kindled in the eyes.
"Galdrafaxi? Yes, of course I can summon him!"
Shiner put two fingers to his mouth and blew a piercing whistle, which was instantly answered by a distant whinny and the beat of approaching hoofs. In no time at all, the horse came into view, first at a joyful gallop, then slowing to a trot and finally a walk.
Galdrafaxi lowered his long, noble head and nuzzled Shiner's hands. Shiner stroked Galdrafaxi's head and kissed him between the ears,

only to nearly lose a tooth as the steed abruptly raised his head again with a sudden snort. The horse backed away, eyes rolling, trotted in a circle, then approached again, his questing nostrils sniffing Shiner from head to foot. Snorri understood the concern and bafflement; Galdrafaxi had an intelligence far beyond that of any normal mount, and it would be foolish to think that his keen senses would fail to detect any change after all that had transpired. His great worry was that Galdrafaxi would reject his reconstituted master and gallop away, but Shiner was stroking the head again and murmuring comforting words.

"My love", Shiner said softly, "do not worry. It is I, but I am somehow changed. I cannot account for it, and I feel dazed. Just listen to this man, this…"

Shiner thought hard for a moment, eyes closed in concentration, then looked up with a grin of delight at having remembered.

"This Snorri. Just do as he tells you."

Snorri had been picking up all the items and stowing them back into the saddle bag, including the three bottles, now empty. He strapped the bag securely to the front of the saddle, and helped Shiner to mount up before taking his own accustomed place behind him. Tightening his knees against the horse's trembling flanks, Snorri cast one last glance over his shoulder and saw that the ashen man-shape and everything that went with it were gone without a trace. He leaned over Shiner's shoulder and gave the command.

"Galdrafaxi, take us to Asgard!"

As Galdrafaxi cantered rapidly, now along a different light-road, the numbing cold was left behind until the temperature was at least tolerable. Still, Snorri thought, it would be good to be somewhere again that was comfortably warm. He felt drained, and worried about Shiner, who slumped half-conscious in front of him and occasionally had to be held to prevent him falling. Snorri's left arm encircled Shiner's waist, while his right hand held the reins – not that Galdrafaxi, excellent horse that he was, needed any guiding or urging. Snorri's sole concern was to get Shiner to a place where he might receive proper treatment, and it never occurred to him to be proud of accomplishing a remarkable magical feat. The last dregs of his energy almost consumed, his head had begun to nod forward onto Shiner's shoulder when a golden glow in the distance indicated that they were finally approaching Asgard. "Hurry, Galdrafaxi!", he gasped, and the horse increased the pace to a gallop. Later on, Snorri would be able only to give a very scant account of his arrival at Asgard's gates, so spent had he been. Trumpets blared, and men in strange garb came running to their assistance. He noticed that they wore odd, three-cornered hats and carried tubular weapons of the kind that had deafened him back in Svartálfheim. There were shouts of "It's Shiner! It's Shiner!", and then the men helped both of them from the saddle. Snorri mumbled "Find help for him... find help... he is back from the dead." He looked at his own hands and noticed that they were nearly transparent, and then he passed out.

# Chapter 10 - Asgard

The bed was wonderfully soft and comfortable, and Snorri turned twice before opening his eyes, unwilling to relinquish sleep. When, eventually, he half-opened his eyes, he saw that the room was gently illuminated by a sepia light, and he wondered whether he was back in Hel. The thought was by no means distressing; he would have been content to carry on sleeping until his soul floated free and went on to whatever new destiny awaited it. He heard someone rise from a chair, the chair making a scraping sound as its feet were pushed back on a wooden floor, and there were footsteps. A door opened, and the footsteps grew fainter at first, paused, then returned in the company of other footsteps. If this was Hel, he thought, it was rather different to his first encounter. Another incongruous thing was that he had a full bladder, something he had not experienced since he died. How could a dead man need to pee? He chuckled at the thought and was pressing his face deeper into the wonderful softness of the pillows when thick, brown drapes were thrown back from a window and bright daylight streamed into the room.
"Are you feeling better now?", asked a female voice, and he turned to see a woman of middle age standing next to his bed. Though not beautiful by any measure, she was not exactly ugly either; merely plain. However, her entire demeanour exuded professionalism and deep knowledge.
"We feared we might lose you", she said, "and that would have been a shame, for you have many questions to answer."
Without further ado she threw back the coverlet and examined Snorri's naked body from top to toe. She placed a hand on his forehead and then over his heart, apparently measuring a pulse. A pulse? The thought astonished Snorri. Somewhat abashed, he asked if he might go outside to relieve himself, and in response she retrieved a wooden bucket from under the bed.
"Do it in this", she said simply, then turned her back to give him a modicum of privacy. Snorri got out of bed and urinated into the bucket. His weak legs trembled, and he tried to will strength into

them, to no avail. When he was done, the woman asked if he would like to take a bath, and Snorri replied that it would be very welcome. She took his arm and led him out of the room and into a corridor.

"My name is Eir", she said. Snorri's eyes widened as she ushered him into another room.

"The Goddess of healing", Snorri said.

"Well remembered, fellow", Eir replied, then pointed towards a long, deep tub made of a white material unfamiliar to Snorri. Two male servants entered the room and assisted him to climb into the tub, their strong arms crossing over his back and under his armpits. They lowered him into the warm water, then took cloths and bars of a strange, cream-coloured substance, washing all the black grit of Niflheim's shores from his body. Eir found a stool to sit on and surveyed his wasted limbs.

"We need to put some meat on you", she said, "but, as I said, there are urgent questions to be answered. Good beef, fowl and greens will do you good, and you can eat those when you dine with Allfather."

Snorri had adopted a luxuriant, supine position, stretching out to his full length with the warm water just below his chin, but now he made the water splash and swirl as he grasped the sides of the bath and pulled himself upright.

"What? I am to meet Allfather? *Odin*? This evening?"

"Who else?", replied Eir with a shrug. "It is he who showed such an interest in you, who commanded your presence. Rumour has it that you have had a long and eventful journey, but it is for Shiner that I am chiefly concerned. I have known him for a long time."

"Shiner!", Snorri exclaimed. "How is he? Can I see him?"

Eir's grey eyes bored into his own.

"He is not well, Snorri Sturluson, and your memories may hold the key to his healing. So finish your bathing now and make haste." And with that, she left. The two manservants helped Snorri to dry off and to dress. The clothes they gave him were of an unfamiliar cut, though not uncomfortable. The shoes were a different matter. They had hard blocks at the heels that threw his weight forward and made it difficult to walk.

"You'll get used to them, Sir", said one of the servants.

The other servant opened the bathroom door to reveal yet another servant, who said simply "This way, if you please Sir", and led him, heels clicking on the hard, marble floor, past multiple guards and along seemingly endless corridors. At one point, Snorri's head swam and he felt exhausted again. He leaned against a wall and his guide seemed embarrassed at having led him too fast. The guide offered him the formal wand that he carried, apparently some kind of symbol of office.

"Would it help Sir to lean on this?", he asked, and Snorri nodded and accepted it gladly. Covering the remaining distance at a rather more considerate pace, they at last arrived at a double door with guards to left and right of it. The guards snapped to attention, holding those bizarre weapons vertically in front of them, then together they opened the double doors.

"Mister Snorri Sturluson, my Lord!", announced the guiding servant and, with a bow and an outstretched arm, ushered Snorri into the chamber. The servant uttered a discreet "Pssst" and clicked his fingers, and Snorri handed him back the wand. The doors clicked shut behind him. Snorri tried not to goggle too obviously as he viewed the scene. Here was such a hall as he had never seen before. The walls were built not of timber but of finely-chiselled ashlar stone and decked with tapestries. The centre of the opposite wall was dominated by an enormous, stone-built fireplace instead of the open hearth in the middle of the floor that he was used to. Before the fireplace stood a long table made of fine, dark wood, and it was covered with many a steaming dish. There were no benches; just two chairs, also made of dark wood, and the seats were covered with some kind of padded, embroidered material, and they had arched backs to lean against. But what took his attention most was the smiling figure who held out his arms in welcome. Odin was tall, but not excessively so, about six feet. Dark hair tumbled to his shoulders in an expansive series of rolled curls. Below the hairline was a high, wide forehead, indicative of great

intelligence, and below that the eyes. The right eye glinted with a pale brightness, like a chip of blue ice; the left was covered by a black leather patch. The nose, cheeks and chin were strongly chiselled, with no fat on them, but to Snorri's surprise he was clean shaven; the long, grey beard that he had expected was absent. Odin was dressed in clothes of a similar cut to those of the servants that Snorri had encountered, but Odin's were entirely in black, apart from the white, lace cravat that swathed the neck. Below the cravat was a black, silk shirt, surmounted by a waistcoat of the same colour, with silver buttons. In turn, these were topped by a broad, open coat, also of silk, that had wide pocket-flaps at the waist and extended down to the mid-thigh. Black knee-breeches clad the lower half, meeting black, silk stockings just below the knee, and the feet were ensconced in shiny black shoes with the kind of raised heels that Snorri had been forced to endure. It was not the image of Allfather that Snorri had expected, but he barely had time to think about it, for Odin had stepped forward and grasped his hands.
"Snorri Sturluson! How glad I am to meet you at last!", said Odin in a deep, resonating voice.
"Pray come and dine with me, and tell me about all your adventures. Please, sit and eat."
A servant appeared out of nowhere and helped Snorri into his seat. Odin sat at the head of the table, not facing Snorri but at his right, to ninety degrees, and this made the arrangement feel more intimate. Servants uncovered the dishes and Snorri, feeling famished, tucked in. As he ate, he began to give an account of his experiences, but Odin seemed distracted, not touching his food but merely sipping at his wine. In the same, charming manner, he held up a hand and Snorri was instantly silenced.
"I am sure that your adventures will be fascinating", said Odin, but for now I must hasten you towards the end – or nearly the end – of your story. What, exactly, happened to Shiner?"
He clicked his fingers, and a secretary appeared carrying a sheaf of papers, a pen and a pot of ink. With another wave of a hand, Odin bade the secretary to be seated.

"Please continue", he said to Snorri. Then, with a smile, "but you can eat at the same time. You look like you need it."

Between mouthfuls, Snorri told of the encounter with Jökulheið, and of Shiner's demise. He spoke of how he had taken out Shiner's thoughts and memory – Odin pressed him for precise details of the procedure he had used - and then begged for Shiner's soul. Finally, he told of how he, in utter desperation, had plundered the saddle bag, conceived the idea of raising Shiner from the dead, and executed the plan. He stopped speaking and looked up from his empty plate. Odin was staring at him with his one eye, and the secretary had stopped writing. A drop of ink fell from the pen and blotted onto the paper. Silence reigned until Odin spoke again in a flat voice.

"You are saying that you raised Shiner from the dead? That you used the remains of his body, his soul, thoughts and memories to reconstitute him?"

Snorri was taken aback. It felt like a rebuke. He began to protest that he had had no other choice, neither for himself or for Shiner, but Odin was not listening. The Allfather was speaking very earnestly to his secretary, and between his excuses, Snorri heard the words

"Did you get all that? Take this information to Eir and Gróa immediately, and send for a Dwarf with the appropriate experience."

The secretary gathered his equipment and hurried away, while Odin sat back in his chair, opened his right eye wide and let out a sigh. Snorri felt very small. He had done his poor best, he thought, and it had been a matter of survival. Now it felt that he was to be blamed for having done everything wrong. He stared at his empty plate until he heard Odin's mellow and utterly charming voice again.

"Do you realise what you have done?"

A morsel of goose-flesh stuck in Snorri's throat. He swallowed hard. "I am sorry, my Lord. I didn't know what else to do."

A gale of laughter filled the room and Odin clapped him hard on the shoulder.

"Snorri Sturluson, I would not have believed it possible that a poor ghost of a mortal could achieve such a feat of necromancy! There is more to you than I could ever have expected! Now, continue with your tale, but start again from the moment you arrived in Hel."

Servants cleared the table, and Odin ordered two armchairs to be pulled up in front of the hearth with a small, round table between them. A pitcher of wine was brought in, and Odin then dismissed all the servants but one, the latter sitting sleepily by the door, only roused when more wine was called for. For the next two hours, Snorri regaled Odin with tales of his travels from Hel to Svartálfheim and thence to Vanaheim, Ljósáfheim, Muspelsheim, Midgard and Niflheim. In between calls for more wine, for which he apparently had an insatiable capacity, Odin occasionally interjected questions, and seemed particularly interested in the relationship between Surt and Jökulheið, Fire and Ice.

"So, in your considered opinion", he asked Snorri, "there is no question of fending off the evil day when these two seek to come together again."

Snorri looked into that glittering eye and then into his wine glass, making sure that his answer was, indeed, his considered opinion.

"No, my Lord", he stated firmly. "I have seen both of them in all their power, and there is nothing that can be done to prevent it. If it is any comfort, they have great love for each other. When the time comes for their mating, you, I, and all the seven other worlds will be swept away. No malice is involved; we will simply be in the way. It is inevitable, but it may not happen for aeons yet."

Odin stretched his legs toward the hearth and put his head back, thinking. He let out a sigh.

"You know, Snorri", he replied in his deep and mellifluous voice, "the drawback of holding great might, great magic, is that you eventually want to have everything under control. Every little thing. Every setback becomes a personal offence, a challenge to be overcome. My brothers and I created this entire system; well, not created it, exactly, but put it all in order. The giants, the Etins, were given their own home after the initial clash. They try to thwart us, now and again, but that's just a healthy relationship between siblings, and they keep us on our toes. They keep us sharp, and when they get too confident Thor, my son, goes out and gives them a good drubbing. We get on well with the Vanir, on the whole, and I actually appreciate their trick of growing Yggdrasil as the framework for the Nine Worlds; I would never have thought of it myself. The Dwarfs and the Light-Elves sort of generated themselves, unbidden; those, too, we have given homes, and very useful jobs they do too. Your world, Snorri, Midgard, is at the centre, and it is our chess-board. All the other worlds impinge upon it. We do not fight each other on our home turf – that would never do – but in that one world that is dominated by mankind. That is why we generated you from two logs, and then Heimdall, also known as Rig, came down to sow the seed of divinity among you. You humans are as we designed you – and more! Sometimes superlatively strong, brave and intelligent, at other times embarrassingly weak, cowardly and foolish, but always unpredictable. That's what makes the game interesting. You can pick your pawn or king, but the piece doesn't always act as bidden, and sometimes a pawn may turn out to be a king."

He turned his face towards Snorri.

"And sometimes Rig's seed comes through undiluted, so that the piece in question has more than a touch of divinity, and becomes a player in its own right."

Snorri did know not what to say. Having heard some of this already from Shiner, he merely nodded and waited for Odin to continue. Odin poured another glass of wine for himself and offered to fill Snorri's glass, but Snorri could not keep up this pace of drinking and declined.

"After I listened to the seeress", Odin went on, "concerning the ultimate downfall of my realm, I determined that I wasn't going to let it happen lying down. I would either avert it, and have victory, or have a death worth a song. I alerted all the Gods and recruited the brave ones, the best of your kind, to fight with the Aesir when the final confrontation comes." He sighed again, and shrugged.

"Now it seems that I underestimated the might and grandeur of the forces we will confront. All will fall. I will die, and perhaps be forgotten, and after that everything will start again."
Snorri sipped from his glass and wondered what words of solace he could give to a morose, mortal God.
"If it is any consolation, my Lord", he said, "that is the fate that we humans are faced with all the time. We are born into life, we grow – if we are lucky and do not die in infancy – we create, we make more humans and, if we are fortunate, our works and deeds are remembered by others, in books, in music, or in the spoken word. We are used to this. The brevity of our lives gives us urgency, knowing that our days are numbered from the point at which we first draw breath."
Odin stared at Snorri with a smile.
"You are a wise man, Snorri", he said, "but now you should sleep. I have asked you many questions. Do you have any questions for me? You had better make them quick ones, for it is late and I have to attend to other business tonight."
"I have many questions, my Lord", Snorri replied, "but you are right, it is late, so I will ask but one. Why do you, why does everything here, look so different to how I had imagined?"
Odin rolled his eye and grinned.
"Oho, I suppose you expected to see someone with a long beard, a broad-brimmed hat and a travel-stained cloak? Or perhaps dressed for battle, with mail and an ornate helmet? That is easily answered. Here in Asgard, we like to move with the times and fashions of Midgard. Have you any idea what year it is now, as men measure the years?"
Snorri thought back and remembered the passage through Midgard.
"Shiner said that time affected us in Midgard", he said. "He said that four hundred years passed while we were traversing that world."
"Indeed", Odin replied, "that many and a few more now. In Midgard it is the year 1700, so I adopt the contemporary fashion. Rather handsome, don't you think?" He stood and spread his arms slightly

so that Snorri could get a good view of the clothes in the firelight. Then Odin did an extraordinary thing that startled Snorri almost as much as the wonders he had seen on his journey so far. He took off his hair, shook it, and placed it atop of a tall pole that was surmounted by a small, wooden disc. While Odin scratched the stubble that remained on his head, Snorri realised that the hair had actually been some kind of headgear, worn for the sake of appearance.

"That's the one part of it that I don't like", Odin continued. "They call it a wig, and it is uncomfortably hot and heavy. Speaking of clothes, how do you like your new suit? I think you look rather dashing, but you should at least tie your hair back with a ribbon and have one of the servants shave off that awful beard."

A knowing look glinted in Odin's eye as he leaned toward Snorri and spoke in a confidential tone.

"I think you will find it impossible here to clothe yourself by dint of imagination and visualisation. Eir tells me that you needed a piss when you woke this afternoon, and you ate like a horse as we dined. Have you not noticed the difference in yourself? Having arrived in Asgard, you are no longer a mere shade. Your body is restored to you."

Odin fished in one of his capacious pockets, brought out a very small, folding knife and opened it.

"Here, prick your thumb with this."

Snorri used the knife's point to prick the ball of his left thumb and was rewarded by a stab of pain. A red bead of blood formed at the site of the wound.

"You see", laughed Odin, "quite your old self again, though a lot younger-looking. I'll instruct the servants to bring you a mirror in the morning so that you can see for yourself."

He passed a hand, palm down, over the wound and it healed at once. With one finger he wiped off the drop of blood, placed it on his tongue, and swallowed with an expression of relish. For a fraction of a second, Snorri saw the dark and handsome features replaced by the head of a wolf. Then the vision was gone, and Snorri wondered how many layers of illusion he was dealing with now. He had no time for further speculation, for the doors were thrown open and the servant who had brought him to the chamber stood silently in profile, clearly awaiting him.

"It has been good to meet you at last, Snorri", said Odin, taking him by the hands and raising him from his chair.

"I won't have time to see you tomorrow, but others will provide you with a small tour that you may find interesting. Sleep well tonight!" And with that, Snorri walked backwards for five paces, bowed, and left the chamber. As the doors closed behind him, he thought he heard the flap of wings and the caw and croak of ravens. With one eyebrow raised in inquiry, the servant again offered him his ceremonial wand, but Snorri declined.

"Thank you", he said, "but I am feeling much stronger now after an excellent meal and good wine."

'Much stronger' was an understatement, he thought to himself as he followed the servant back to his bedchamber. He felt wonderful.

Bright sunlight illuminated the room as the curtains were drawn back from the window, and Snorri sat up and rubbed his eyes. A male servant, dressed in the now familiar red, white and black livery of Asgard, stood by the window, a towel draped over his left forearm.

"Good morning, Sir", the servant said cheerfully, "I trust you slept well. Your bath is already drawn. Is there anything in particular that you would like for breakfast?"

Snorri yawned and stretched his arms as he swung his legs over the side of the bed. His feet met a mat covered with tufts of wool, and a pair of woven slippers were also at the bedside. He slipped them on, retrieved the bucket from under the bed and relieved himself.

"No, thank you", he replied. "I will be happy to be surprised at whatever is available."

The servant nodded and led him to the adjoining room where a bath full of steaming water awaited him as on the previous day, though no other servants were present this time. Snorri scratched his tangled locks and felt at the long beard that fell to his collar bones.

"Do you think I might have a trim?", he asked.

"Certainly, Sir", replied the servant. "How short?"

"I would like to lose all the face hair. Shave it all off. As for the head hair, please do as you see fit; I would like to fit in with the current fashion."

The servant smiled, drew up a high-backed chair and, from a cupboard, brought out scissors, a straight razor and a comb.

"A very good choice, Sir. It would be best to perform the task before your bath. Please sit."

For the next half-hour, Snorri sat as the servant trimmed away the beard, lathered and shaved his face, and combed and trimmed the hair of his head. Then he climbed into the bath, needing no assistance now, and soaked in the warm water. The servant handed him a bar of soap and showed him how to use it, then soaped and rinsed his hair and combed it again. After drying himself off, Snorri allowed the servant to help him don the still unfamiliar clothes, noting that a fresh shirt, underwear and stockings had been laid out for him. Eventually, the servant pulled a tall mirror in front of him, and Snorri was able for the very first time to survey himself in his entirety. The image took his breath away. It was like looking at a different man altogether. The eyes and nose were the same, he supposed, but the face resembled that of an unbearded youth. Not only that, but he had a full head of brown hair, instead of grey hair surrounding a bald pate, and the hair was tied back neatly with a black ribbon. He tried to assess the age of the man reflected in the mirror, and judged him to be thirty at the most. Less than half the age he had been when he died in Midgard. The servant's face appeared behind his shoulder in the reflection.

"A handsome image, Sir, if I may say so. Would you care to take breakfast now?"

After breakfast, Snorri sat back and rubbed his full belly. "I am indeed in Paradise", he thought. Had he chosen to specify his requirements, he might have called for some butter on his bread, a helping of pickled meat, and a pint of small beer. Instead, he had been served fried kidneys, bacon, eggs, and toasted, buttered slices

of white bread. He sipped at the drink that they called 'coffee'. He had found it bitter and unpalatable at first, until his servant suggested that he should add a brown, granular substance called 'sugar' to sweeten it. Other servants, most of them female, were clearing away the silver and pewter tableware when a man entered the room, removed his broad-brimmed hat, and stood by the door. The man's face was deeply tanned and bore a long scar on the right side. He wore a long, dark-green coat with brass buttons, and the coat was surmounted by a kind of short cape that covered the shoulders. Below the coat, the feet and lower legs were covered by black, mud-spattered riding boots. He might, thought Snorri, have been an old warrior, a poacher, a gamekeeper, or a pirate. Perhaps all of these. Snorri's manservant leaned down and spoke quietly.
"That is Wulfhere, Sir. He is to be your guide for today."
Snorri dabbed remnants of grease from his lips with a serviette, brushed crumbs from his waistcoat, and walked to the door. Wulfhere simply nodded a greeting, said "Sir" and led him outside to where two geldings, one black and the other piebald, stood tethered. Without speaking, Wulfhere untethered both horses, held the reins of the piebald while Snorri mounted, then mounted the black one. Without a word, he set off at a steady trot. Snorri tagged along behind at first, but then urged his horse forward so that he rode alongside Wulfhere.
"So where are we off to today?", he asked.
"The master thought you might like to see Valhalla", replied Wulfhere in a gruff tone, but did not elaborate. Snorri could not place his accent. Nevertheless, he felt as giddy as a small child going to a fair. Valhalla! The place where Odin's share of the chosen slain were taken after battle by Valkyries, forever to feast and practise fighting until they were called to the final showdown at Ragnarök! This promised to be exciting. As they rode, they passed a cart coming the other way. The carter touched his cocked, three-cornered hat in salute, and Wulfhere nodded in return. Snorri was reminded that different fashions prevailed these days, and a question formed in his mind.

"I expect things will be done differently now", he said. "Will the warriors be using those…" he searched for an appropriate phrase, "those infernal bang-sticks that I saw in Dark-Elf Home and at the gate? Instead of swords and spears, I mean."

A sardonic smile briefly crossed Wulhere's tanned features, and he gave a small laugh.

"Muskets, you mean? No, Sir. I think you will find they like to keep things traditional in that part of Asgard."

Their path took them through a broad, pleasant dale that gradually rose towards higher ground. Sheep and cattle grazed in the adjacent fields, and the beck to their left was bordered by oaks, willows and alders Along the way, they passed many splendid mansions and palaces, one of which commanded a magnificent view of the entire valley. It was built in a style familiar to Snorri, with a roof of oaken shingles and crossed beams terminating in dragon heads at the gable above the doorway.

"That palace is well placed!", said Snorri.

Wulfhere glanced up at it.

"Indeed, Sir. It is called Breiðablik, meaning 'Broad View'. The home of Master Baldr and his wife Nanna."

Snorri had to take a moment or two to digest this information. The mythology with which he had been familiar said that Baldr had been slain by a mistletoe shaft, and that he resided now in Hel. He sought for a way to present his question diplomatically.

"So… does Master Baldr live there still?", he asked.

Wulfhere rode on and raised his eyes to the sky, as if trying to ascertain whether it might rain that day. On the other hand, thought Snorri, he might be indicating that he was tiring of his questions, and it occurred to him that Odin might have chosen a more conversational guide for the day.

"It… is difficult to say, Sir", Wulfhere replied. "For as long as I can remember, none are allowed near the place. I once had the impertinence to ask the same question, and Allfather answered me with a riddle. Something about a Dutchman having a cat in a box, and nobody being able to tell whether it was alive or not. I could make neither head nor tail of it, and I pay it no heed now."

# Chapter 11 - Valhalla

Presently, as the ground rose, they came within sight of a magnificent hall. Its walls were made of long spears, and its roof was tiled with shields. Before it was a broad, grassy meadow on which two opposing lines comprising hundreds of warriors faced each other. Already some bodies lay on the green sward. Wulfhere reined his horse to a halt, dismounted, and took the reins of Snorri's piebald as he also dismounted.
"I'll just wait here, Sir, while you have a look around", he said, and then went away, leading the horses, to talk with one of the yellow-tabarded, supervising captains. Excited and on foot, Snorri approached the rear of the nearer battle-line. The line was four-deep, and all the warriors were clashing their spears or swords against their shields, chanting battle songs and hurling insults at the opposing line. Suddenly a horn blew, and the lines surged forward at a steady trot. So this was it, thought Snorri, the daily battle between the chosen, the *Einherjar*, who would fight, die, be called back to life again, and then feast together in that glittering hall! As he trotted behind them, the closer line maintained its cohesion, shields overlapping, while the further line's attack was more ragged in its enthusiasm. With a tremendous clash of shields, the forces met, and then there was a great deal of pushing, hacking and stabbing. Here and there, and with increasing frequency, came cries of 'Ooooh!' and 'Aaargh!' and 'Oh you bugger, you got me this time'. Men fell to the ground, and then the opposite line broke and ran away uphill towards the great hall, pursued by the warriors that Snorri had stood behind. He turned to look around at the prostrate corpses, only to see them shuffling towards each other or leaning on their elbows to watch the rout. A group of them gathered in a circle, spread a cloth, and brought out some dice. Of blood there was not a trace. Their weapons lay beside them on the grass, and Snorri – asking permission first – picked up a sword. Carefully, he ran a finger over its edge. It was not even sharp. He handed it back to the owner, and looked at a spear. Its point was blunt and rounded. Some of the swords even had layers of cloth tied around

their blades, and a fearsome-looking axe turned out to be made entirely of wood. He sat down next to a ring of dice-players.
"Mind if I join you?", he asked.
One of the players, chewing on a halm of grass, tossed the dice, and said "Damn!" at the outcome.
"Who the fuck are you?", asked the warrior, looking up at Snorri's shaven face.
"I'm sorry, Snorri said", I didn't intend to interrupt your game. My name is Snorri Sturluson."
The warrior's eyes opened wide, and all of his companions gave a gasp.
"What, THE actual Snorri Sturluson?", he asked incredulously. "The Boss said you might be dropping in to see us. Hey, lads! Gather round! Snorri's here."
To Snorri's amazement, all the fallen warriors began to crawl towards him. Some even stood up and walked at first but, catching severe frowns from the supervising captains, got down on the ground again and crawled. Soon he was surrounded by a ring of about one hundred mail-clad warriors. A grizzled sergeant pushed through the crowd on his knees and elbows, and shook Snorri's hand.
"Pleased to meet you, Mister Snorri!", he said. "You're the biz, a real legend among us lads. Everyone here knows you kept the legend alive. If it wasn't for you, nobody would know about us and all the trouble we go to."
This was met by a hundred comments of 'Yeah!', 'Not half!' and enthusiastic nods. The sergeant continued.
"If it wasn't for you giving us a good write-up, nobody would ever have heard about us Chosen Men! Never a mention for the past four hundred years. Down there in Midgard these days, they're mostly into Gideon and Joshua, whoever they were, and hardly a one comes here."
Snorri sat down on the grass, arms encircling his knees, looking at the many expectant, smiling faces. Clearly, he had to give some response.

"I'm glad to have given you the fame that you deserve", he said, and this raised an immediate cheer.

"You chosen ones, you Einherjar, will be remembered until the end of the world!", he continued, and this raised even greater applause. Those who had sustained light wounds, or here and there a broken limb or rib, lay on the grass and beat their weapons against their shields, and even the supervising captains nodded sidelong to each other with grim, satisfied smiles and clapped. Men were coming back down the hill after the rout of the opposing side and, not wishing to let things get too much out of hand, the captains blew on their horns and gave commands.

"All right, then!", shouted one in a powerful voice. "Nobody told you to stop fighting! Those of you are not really hurt, back on your feet and form up! Those with wounds report to the Valkyries."

A groan came from the crowd of warriors. Some stood up again and stretched their limbs, others lay prone or supine, feigning death until they received a sharp kick to the ribs. The warrior with whom Snorri had first spoken gathered up his dice and casting-cloth, stowed them in his pouch and, with a shrug, joined the host as it formed up again. Two of the captains in their yellow vests stood in the middle and conferred. Snorri could not hear what they said, but in the end they nodded agreement and one of them raised his voice to address the waiting fighters.

"OK, switch round. The side that was downhill last time, will move up towards the hall and attack downhill. Those who were uphill last time, move downhill a bit and form up facing the hall. And remember, don't make the same mistake as last time and get impetuous. The side that keeps its shield-wall together generally wins. Right, move off. Smartly now!"

With a clattering of arms, the warriors wearily changed positions, interpenetrating each other's line without fuss. Here and there, they exchanged greetings and clapped each other on the shoulder. Then it all began again. Lines were drawn up, horns blew, and again there was the clamour of shields and blades meeting. This time the tussle lasted longer. Men gave cries of agony and fell to the ground, to be replaced by someone from a rear rank, but eventually one side broke and was pursued across the field by the other. A yelling warrior ran at Snorri, eyes wide and sword raised, then recognised him and swerved aside.

"Sorry, Mister Snorri!" he shouted, and was gone. Snorri was left among a field of corpses as the battle receded downhill. Once again, however, the corpses were moving, gathering in circles, and bringing out dice and flagons of ale. He joined a group and watched their play.

"Err... I'm glad to see that you are not really hurt", he ventured, "but how does all this work? I thought you died in daily battle, and that Odin raised you from the dead to feast together in the evening?"

There was a shocked silence. Dice tumbled from a hand, ignored.

"Die?", said a warrior. "No, that's not the way of it now."

The other players laughed in agreement. Snorri felt quite confused, and persisted.

"I... I saw all the blunt weapons... the swords bound in layers of cloth. And you fall down before you are really hurt. What does it all mean?"

The grizzled, scarred warriors glanced at each other and looked at their feet, but one of them, a thin-faced man with a scar across his forehead, spoke up.

"Have you ever been slashed or stabbed with a sword?"

Snorri's fingers went unconsciously to the sites of his own death-wounds.

"Um, yes... that was how I died."

"Bloody hurts, doesn't it?", continued the thin-faced man. "Now imagine that, every day for... how long? Every day for a hundred years? You soon get tired of that. So we all agreed to blunt our weapons or bind them up so nobody gets hurt too much. You see, you might get a wound that's bad but not fatal. Not just a little nick, but a really nasty one that has your guts spilling on the ground. You going to put up with that the whole day until the final horn is blown, and we can all go in to supper? Not if you can help it. Now, whenever we feel a thrust or a tap, we shout 'Aargh!' and go down. Saves everybody a lot of grief."

Snorri had to admit that he had a point.

"And what about the feasting and drinking at the end of the day?", he asked. "Has that changed too?"

"Not half!", replied another warrior. "When I first got here, it was boiled pork and mead every day of the week, with two helpings on Wednesday. Pork and mead, pork and mead. It sounds alright to a young warrior who's often wondered where his next meal was coming from, but take it from me, it soon palls. So, a couple of hundred years ago, we went on strike and refused to pick up a blade until things improved. Now we get a regular spread with a lot of choice – beef, lamb, fish, you name it, some greens, and five kinds of bread to choose from. And you don't have to drink mead neither, if you don't want it. You can drink strong ale, small ale, milk, whey, water: whatever you like. Matter of fact, a lot of the lads have gone on the wagon on account of the hangovers we used to get."

There was a stir behind Snorri, and he turned to see that a messenger had arrived. Wulfhere and the umpires had gathered around him and were chattering animatedly. To judge from their smiles, it seemed the messenger had brought good news. Wulfhere strode over, leading their horses.

"Time to go, Sir", he said, "we are called to another visit."

Snorri stood, dusted off his breeches, and profusely thanked the warriors for their conversation. Many muddied hands, some scratched and bruised, were wiped on trousers and offered to him with mumbled appreciation, until he eventually had to give a wave to all of them and mount his horse.

"Come and stay for supper next time!", called a voice as he rode away.

They trotted away from the meadow and the shining hall, rejoining the path by which they had come. It was well past noon, and Snorri's stomach gurgled, perhaps prompted by the thought of supper with the *Einherjar*. Wulfhere must have heard it, for he reached into a pocket, drew out a hunk of bread, and offered it to him. Snorri accepted it gratefully and chewed on it, wishing that he had something to wash it down with. They turned into another lane, and rode on at a walk for a mile or two between high-banked hedges and under the greater shade offered by spreading oaks and beeches. Blackbirds and thrushes sang, and the afternoon was altogether pleasant except at one point when they were surrounded by a swarm of flies.

"Bugger off, Loki", muttered Wulfhere, singling out one fly for a swat, but missing. "Tha'll get nowt out o' me."

The flies were left behind. Snorri was starting to resent Wulfhere's taciturn nature. As a man who had dealt in words all his life, he loved to talk, but stubbornly felt inclined to deny his guide the pleasure of a brusque response, so he simply continued to follow and enjoyed the passing scenery. They crossed a beck at a ford, mud spattering on Snorri's shoes and stockings as they crossed. It irked him that his newly acquired finery should be spoiled thus, but then he reflected that it was he, rather than the clothing, who was becoming spoiled. It was a petty thing. Had he not but recently braved the dangers of ultimate fire and ice, nearly losing his existence on the shores of Niflheim? The irritation was borne away by the thought, supplanted by a soaring joy at his present circumstances, and his head swam like that of a youth whose love has been requited. His innately poetic nature took over, and he spontaneously composed an ode to joy and sang it aloud. The birds took up the song, carrying it away into the ether. Many years later, it was to drizzle down and be taken up by a German poet and set to the music of a German composer, neither of whom was aware of its origin. Even Wulfhere was moved a little, and allowed himself a wry grin.

# Chapter 12 – A Reunion

After they had crossed the ford, the ground gradually began to rise and become more open. The sandy path traversed broad pasture in zig-zag fashion, unbounded by hedges, though the pasture was dotted here and there with mature trees, and there were entire copses that were fenced off to protect them against the grazing sheep. The sun was sinking towards the horizon, and clouds rose from the south with the promise of a rainy evening. Overhead, a kite flew, seeking some morsel of carrion. At the top of the hill was a simple hall, built of wood and roofed with thatch. Under the eaves of the wall was a verandah, and on it Snorri could make out people sitting on benches, talking and drinking. One of them looked familiar. Snorri squinted his eyes.
"Is that… is that Shiner?", he asked, bringing his horse alongside Wulfhere's.
"Indeed it is", said Wulfhere with a smile, "and that is the reason we came quickly away from Valhall."
Snorri's heart surged, and with a whoop he dug his heels into the flanks of his mount to make it canter, then again to bring it to a full gallop across the remaining furlong until he reined it in abruptly before the hall and leapt from the saddle. On the verandah, Shiner stood up with the broadest of grins, and Snorri raced into his welcoming embrace. They hugged hard and long, and when they faced each other again, both had tears in their eyes.
"Are you mended? Are you hail?", Snorri enquired, hands still clutching his friend's forearms as his gaze went from head to toe and back again. The loving smile remained on Shiner's face, despite the tears in the eyes.
"That I am", he replied, "thanks to the best of care, but above all thanks to you. Two of the present company, I gather, you have already met", and he indicated Eir, goddess of healing, and the Dwarf Fundinn. Both of them beamed and nodded, and Snorri bowed his head in return.
"The other", Shiner continued, "is my wife, Gróa. She also had a part in my healing, for she is skilled in such matters."

A small woman stepped forward to stand at Shiner's side, putting an arm around his waist. Her hair was blonde, streaked with grey, and her eyes were bright blue. She nodded to Snorri, then looked up sideways to her husband, her eyes shining with adoration. Booted feet resounded on the short flight of steps leading from ground to verandah, and Wulfhere stood behind Snorri, having handed the horses into the care of a groom.

"And I see you have already met my friend Wulfhere!", said Shiner. "Well, we all could not wish for better company. It looks like it is about to rain, so let us go inside and exchange news."

Even as he spoke, raindrops driven by the southerly wind began to spatter on the verandah as the last rays of the sun went down, and they all went indoors. The hall's interior, Snorri noticed, was comfortable rather than luxurious, and there were many features that were familiar to Snorri as Shiner proudly showed him around. Boxed beds with shutters arrayed the walls closest to the fireplace, and a large table with benches occupied the centre of the hall, but instead of a central hearth there was the type of stone hearth with a chimney that Snorri had seen at Odin's palace. They sat down at the table and, presently, a servant brought a large jug of wine, earthenware goblets, and a platter with a selection of hors d'oeuvres. Shiner raised his goblet in a toast.

"Here's to Snorri, our guest and my saviour!", he said, and Snorri blushed as they all toasted his health. He nodded, and drank also.

"That was a truly astonishing feat of magic that you performed, Snorri", said Gróa. "Thank you for bringing my husband back to me. Your deed is the talk of Asgard."

"Indeed it is", agreed Eir. "I can heal almost anyone, while they still have life, but bringing someone back from the dead is a power reserved for Odin and the most powerful of sorcerers. I should like to hear how you accomplished it."

Once again, Snorri had to recount the events that had taken place on that grey and dreadful shore, ending with Shiner's return to life, his confused state of mind, and their exhaustion when they arrived at the gates of Midgard. He carefully left out Shiner's fatal infatuation with the Snow Maiden.

"But you are now fully healed, I see", he ended, "and mightily glad I am. Others can take credit for your complete restoration to health." There was a silence as the assembled company digested the amazing story, until Fundinn spoke.

"After you had told Odin exactly what you had done, he sent for me, and I was able to set straight some of your rough and inexperienced work. Don't get me wrong: you did a fine job with Shiner's soul, mind and memory, Snorri, and without the proper tools, too. All I had to do was repair some of the kinks and breaks in the threads of his memories, and a couple of small dents in his cognition. That's the proper work of a Dwarf soul-smith, and a master at that. You must have been paying close attention at our place to get even the basics right. I'd offer you an apprenticeship in our guild, but I'm afraid that's reserved for Dwarfs."

Snorri smiled, warmed by this huge compliment, but something else was plucking the strings of his curiosity.

"One thing that I still don't understand", he said, "is how I had the wherewithal to perform the magic in the first place. The instructions and the stave were there in your book of magic; as for elaborating on those… well, let's just say that necessity is the mother of invention. I had to do something, otherwise I, too, would have remained in that awful place. What I don't understand is why you carried that bag with your heart and ashes with you, never letting it out of your sight. You gave me the clue when you said it contained your body, but I didn't really understand until I opened it. I have thought on it many times since, but I can't really make sense of it."

Shiner was about to answer, but the servant came and announced that dinner was about to be served.

"Let's leave that story until after dinner", Shiner said with a wink.

After they had eaten a good repast, comfortable, high-backed chairs had been arrayed by the fireplace, accompanied by very small tables with room for a goblet and a jug, but little else. Snorri leaned back in his chair, rubbed his stomach, and undid a few buttons of his waistcoat. Not for the first time since he came to Asgard, he

reflected that it was pleasant to know again the delight of a full belly. And, for that matter (he thought back to the afternoon, when a crust of bread had been welcome), the opposite, the pangs of hunger. The one went with the other, two sides of the same coin, and he remembered the promises of the Christian Bible that he had been brought up with – a Heaven in which there was never any need or suffering, or, conversely, any pleasure in their opposites. Only an eternal sameness and absence of sensation. He wondered how he could have ever found that an attractive proposition, and started to doze in happy satiation until the servant placed a wooden bowl on his side-table. The bowl contained finely-shredded, dry, brown leaves and a small device that appeared to be made of white pot. He picked it up and turned it in his hands, noting that it had a small bowl at one end with a tiny aperture in its bottom. The aperture looked like it led to the projecting pipe, which also had an aperture at its end. Thinking it to be some kind of whistle, he put it to his mouth and blew, but no sound came out. His confusion was increased when he saw that Shiner, Wulfhere and Fundinn were taking similar devices and stuffing them with the brown leaves. They lit the leaves with long, waxen tapers of a kind that Snorri had never seen before, sucked on the pipes, and blew out clouds of blue-grey smoke with an expression of pleasure. The ladies smiled but lowered their heads and devoted their attention to their knitting. Wulfhere laughed, a low, deep chuckle.
"It's called 'smoking', Sir, and it's all the rage in Midgard these days. Here, let me help you. Most of the trick lies in knowing how tight to pack the leaves."
Taking Snorri's pipe, he took a generous pinch of leaves and pressed them judiciously down into the bowl."
"If I may make so free, Sir?", he asked and, without further ado, he lit the surface of the leaves and sucked on the pipe's stem until a small glow came from the bowl. He breathed out smoke, and handed the pipe to Snorri after wiping the stem on his sleeve. Snorri gingerly took the pipe, sucked on it, and inhaled, only to be assaulted by an immediate coughing fit and a feeling of nausea.

Small dots of light danced around his field of vision as he wiped tears from his eyes.

"For Od's sake", he exclaimed, coughing, "you do this for pleasure?", and this was met by a gale of laughter. Shiner kicked off his shoes, stretched his legs, and took another tug on his own pipe.

"As Wulfhere said, it's the rage in Midgard these days. Rather pleasurable, but very addictive for mortals. He introduced me to it, since I came to my senses, but I expect it plays havoc on mortal lungs."

Snorri decided that this particular experience was one that did not attract him further, and laid his pipe down on the table. He took a sip of wine to ease his dry throat.

"Speaking of mortal lungs, I have to press you again on the matter of that bag, the one that contained, as you put it, 'your body'. Without it, I could not have restored you, but why were you carrying it, even into Niflheim?"

Shiner took another couple of puffs on his pipe, and drank some more wine, brows knitted in earnest thought.

"Snorri, my friend", he said, "you did more than save my life. You brought me back to life, so I owe you an explanation, and I will tell you a story that none has heard before, save my wife. Even Wulfhere, my friend, has never heard the story before."

He put down his pipe, took another sip of wine, and began his tale.

"You know me as Shiner, but I have many names. I am called Skírnir, Orvandil, Earandel and Hermod, among others. I was born a mortal, long ago, and I devoted myself to magic from my seventh incarnation. I travelled the world in search of knowledge, from the rites of the Saami people to the libraries of Egypt and Greece. Eventually, I learned to hold on to my memories, from life to life. I saw kingdoms and empires rise and fall. Even in life, I travelled seven of the Nine Worlds in shadow-form, lying down on my bed, hardly breathing, and spoke with the Gods. In the north, I came to be renowned as a Rune-master. When I died for the last time, the Gods told me that I was done with mortal life. They found me useful, and I was to be their messenger, a task that I have done my best to fulfil. When last I died, I happened to be in Egypt, and the people there mummified my body according to their local custom. A magician of a poor, dabbling sort later found the grave and made the mistake of trying to compel me to do his will, using my body parts. Needless to say, being summoned I showed him the error of his ways. I went easy on him, only temporarily depriving him of his sanity, for it was the kind of thing I might have done myself once. Then I took my mummified body and burned it, apart from the heart, and I stowed the ashes and the shrivelled heart in my saddle bag, to be forever in my own safekeeping. And that is why you found them on that cheerless shore, and were able to revive me. The Norns work in mysterious ways."

Gróa, without looking up from her knitting, smiled.

"That would account for the restoration of the little toe on your left foot", she said. "You lost it to frostbite, returning with Thor from Jötunheim, remember? And, since Snorri raised you from your old bones, it is back again."

Shiner frowned, groped though his stocking at his left foot, then raised his head in amazement.

"By the gods, you are right! I had not noticed it myself!"

Gróa simply smiled again, put her knitting down on her lap and took a sip of wine.

"I noticed it when you first came back, when we lay in bed together, and you rubbed your feet against my legs. A wife notices such small details."

She suddenly raised her head and cast her eyes about the room and to the rafters, lips pressed hard together in a vain effort to hide the woe that she felt. Tears sprang from her eyes, and her throat bobbed.

"I do not know how much longer I can bear you taking these risks, my love", she sobbed, and wiped the springing tears away with the tips of her fingers. Her chest heaved.

"It was bad enough to see you in danger, time and again, and a relief that you came back to me with only the loss of a toe on that occasion. But this time, you nearly died. No, you *did* die! And it was only because of Snorri's quick wit that you came back at all. Odin had no business to send you on such a forlorn mission!"

Shiner began to protest sympathetically, but Gróa rose, dropped her knitwork on her chair, and hurried away, weeping, to the kitchen. Eir got up and followed her, and the kitchen door closed behind them.

Snorri, Shiner, Wulfhere and Fundinn, suddenly deprived of female company and unsure of how to deal with such emotion, shifted uneasily in their seats. Snorri picked up his clay pipe and toyed with the idea of lighting it again. The others smoked theirs, and an uneasy silence settled upon them. Fundinn was the first to speak.

"You have to admit she has a point", he said. "The Boss takes your willingness an awful lot for granted."

Wulfhere exhaled tobacco smoke, raised his eyebrows, and nodded in agreement. Shiner only shrugged, said "Yes, well...", but did not continue. Snorri noted for the first time that Fundinn looked different, and found a way to break out of this embarrassing impasse.

"Master Fundinn", he exclaimed, "where is your beard? And what is that... what do they call it?... That wig on your head?"

And indeed, Fundinn looked considerably less like the classical image of a Dwarf. The long beard was entirely absent, and he wore a small, powdered wig on his head. The buttoned waistcoat and knee-breeches suited him rather well, Snorri thought. Fundinn raised a hand to scratch his bald head beneath the wig, then stroked the stubble on his chin.

"Aye, well, you have to move with the times. Would you look at yourself, Mister Snorri? All decked out like a gentleman of – what year is it now in Midgard? – of 1700? But I'll tell you what, now that my services are no longer required here, and once I've had a wee holiday at Shiner's expense, and taken my fee from Allfather, I'll be back down with the lads in my leather apron, beard restored, and doing some honest work again."

He chuckled and drank a generous gulp from his goblet, and the others laughed too. Snorri relaxed and looked at Wulfhere.

"And what is your story, my taciturn guide?", he asked. Wulfhere rolled his eyes, turned his head, and made a wry face before answering.

"Had anyone but you had the impertinence to ask", he replied, "I should have told them that it was none of their business. I keep myself to myself, do as I am bidden, and keep a very small ring of companions but, as you have saved the dearest of those, I shall open myself to you. I was born near York, in the north of England, an Englishman partly of Danish ancestry. My family kept to the old ways, d'you understand? We went to Church as little as we could decently get away with, and we held our rites in the woods and on the hills, away from prying eyes. It was a hard life, and I stole a sheep and was caught. They were going to hang me, but I got away and fled to York, where I lived as a thief and trickster. Then came the bastard William of Normandy, and the north rose in rebellion. I knew then that I had to pick my side, and I joined the rebels. We fought them, and we fought hard, but it was no use. In the end, my band was trapped in a gill somewhere up in the dales, with Norman horsemen before us and Norman archers shooting down on us from the cliffs. I died then, sword in hand, and for my heathen bravado I was carried away to Valhalla. Well, Sir, you've seen what Valhalla is like, and I can only say that I was bored of it in pretty short order. Fortunately, along came Mister Shiner and, seeing that I had potential, he took me away from that and made me his apprentice. He is my master, and also my best friend, and it is thanks to him that I have some small status here. When he has need of me, I accompany him on his quests. Otherwise, I have my own small cottage down the hill from here, and lead a comfortable life."

The three smokers puffed contentedly on their pipes. Snorri sucked briefly at the stem of his unlit pipe, gave up, and laid it down again. "And what is your story, Snorri?", asked Wulfhere. "We have told you ours, and I, for one, am very curious to know why Allfather saw fit to send you and my master on such a chase around Yggdrasil, even to the perilous regions never visited by anyone in his right mind."

Snorri cringed under the gaze of six piercing eyes, for Shiner and Fundinn clearly shared Wulfhere's curiosity. Especially Shiner, who had so far performed his mission without question. To maintain his dignity and give himself some time to think, Snorri re-lit his pipe, sucked on it without inhaling, and managed to blow out a stream of smoke without coughing.

"I... I cannot comment on Odin's purpose", he replied. He was about to continue when Gróa and Eir returned from the kitchen and resumed their seats, Gróa first taking up her knitwork again and kissing her husband on the forehead.

"I was but a simple skald", he said, "though a good one, if I say it myself. I was born of good family, and came to attend the courts of rival kings in Norway. I took a great interest in our traditional forms of poetry, and wished to preserve the poetic skills that I felt were being lost, so I wrote a short book of instruction on the subject. I was raised as a Christian, but I found that I could not adequately explain the forms and the kennings without reference to the lore of Heathen times. To be honest, I was rather fascinated by all that, the old tales that were still told about gods, giants, elves and mortal heroes, and I perhaps got carried away and wrote rather more about them than I need have done. I tried to be careful not to present the old stories as truth – that would have brought me a lot a trouble from the Church and its priests! – and invented explanations that were acceptable, such as the Aesir being so-called because they came from Asia. But it was not from the Churchmen that I had to fear in the end, but from my rash involvement in secular politics. Being born of a respected family, I might have had some influence in a civil war that loomed in Iceland. I tried to flee my destiny and settle back into obscurity, but I was pursued. Men came in the night and slew me in my bath-house, and the next thing I knew was that I was lying in Hel, where Shiner found me and took me on our late journey."

"That explains something, at least", said Shiner. "Allfather informed me that you had written something, that you had got a lot of things wrong and omitted much, and that it was necessary to show you the facts. Though why it should be so important to correct the author of a book, he did not say. Perhaps we shall find out tomorrow."

At these words, Snorri experienced a frisson of excitement, mixed with trepidation. He was keen to learn more about the mysteries of the multiverse, but his heart sank at the thought of the additional demands that might be placed upon him. Having been through so much already, he had begun to hope that this was the journey's end, where he could finally live in obscure comfort, and he said as much to his companions. Wulfhere gave a cynical laugh. Shiner, clearly still tired, shook his head slightly and gazed into the fire. The ladies pretended to be engrossed in their knitting. Fundinn gave a snort, and spoke for all them.

"Aye, lad, you do well to be wary of Odin. He gives much, but there is always a price to pay. He'd like to own your soul, but he cannot do that. No matter whether you are Man, Elf, Wane, Ase or Etin, everyone owns his own soul forever; it is your *Odal*. But he can rent it for a while, by contract, if you are unwise enough to make a binding agreement with him. And that 'while' can last a thousand years or more. So be careful what you agree to, and set your fee wisely, and never, *ever*, allow that slippery Loki to be his mediator, for then you are sure to come unstuck. As for me, I'm happy to be doing the small work that I do in Dwarf-home. It has been a pleasure to come here to help with Shiner's mending, but in the morning I will be off again and back to the work I love."

Snorri pondered his words while the rest stretched and yawned, and Gróa and Eir packed their knitting away into bags. It was late, and Snorri, sensing that the evening was at its end, drank the last dregs from his goblet. Before they rose from their chairs, Shiner, who had been silent for much of the time, spoke.

"Odin is my Lord", he said quietly. "I will not speak ill of him, for I have gained much from him in the years since I quit mortal life. In mortal incarnation, there was nothing more that I could learn, but now I learn from every mission that he assigns to me. He is like the wind, blowing you this way and that. Sometimes he blows softly, from the direction that you want, and makes your journey smooth. At other times, he blows like the gale, either hindering you or driving you to an unknown and unexpected destination. But you can fight against him, and set your own course. He respects that, and he values those who resist his will, for they are strong."

Gróa, knowing that her husband was still not fully recovered from the hurt he had sustained, gently took his arm and ushered him towards the box-bed against the inner wall of the hall, closest to the hearth. Wulfhere showed Snorri to his own bed, and then all was still for the night.

Next morning, they had just finished their breakfast, and were drinking the last of the coffee, when a knock came at the door.
"Always perfect timing", said Shiner, "you can rely on him for that."
At the door, a herald announced the expected news that their presence, Snorri's and Shiner's, was requested at the palace. Wulfhere and Shiner's own groom already stood outside, holding the reins of the horses, Galdrafaxi and the piebald that had been loaned to Snorri. After the rainy night, a damp mist hung over the pasture that extended below the hall, suffused with gold from the rising sun. The darker copses and isolated trees were mere blurs, and out of the mist issued plaintive bleats from hidden sheep. Just as Snorri was about to mount, Gróa came to him bearing a heavy, brown coat that had two extra layers attached below the collar to cover the shoulders.

"It's a cold morning, Snorri", she said brightly, "you should wear this to keep you warm. It's a new one that I got for my husband, but he says he is not used to the new fashions yet."

She handed it to him, and Snorri gave his grateful thanks as he donned it. Gróa then turned to her husband and hugged him, kissing his cheek.

"Now you come back quickly", she ordered him, "for you still need time and care to recover your full strength. And whatever that old user tells you to do next, whatever mission he has in mind for you, I want to be the first to hear about it."

Shiner grinned and hugged her to his chest.

"My love, I rather think that he only has a pleasurable day of sight-seeing in mind but, if anything changes, I assure you that you will be the first to know."

Somewhat, but not entirely, mollified, Gróa released her husband and stood back as Shiner and Snorri mounted their horses.

Wulfhere handed the reins of Galdrafaxi to Shiner, his head level with Shiner's waist.

"Is there anything you'll be wanting from me today, Sir?", he asked.

Shiner shook his head.

"No, nothing in particular. You can have the day off, but keep your eyes and ears open as usual."

The herald gave a meaningful cough, and the trio set off on their trip, Snorri and Shiner waving their goodbyes to Gróa, Eir and Fundinn as they stood on the verandah. Somewhere in the mist, a raven croaked.

# Chapter 13 – Mimir's Well

With the herald in the lead, they rode uphill at an easy walk. After a mile, they emerged from the clinging mist and Sunna's rays shone on them, bright and warm. Snorri eased off the heavy coat and hung it in front of his saddle. He wondered whether it was the same sun that had shone on Midgard, in Vanaheim and also in Ljósálfheim. After all, he now knew that a small and insignificant star illuminated the world that he had, until quite recently, inhabited; surely it could not be the same one? After some cogitation, he decided, accurately, that the concept of Sunna, if not the actual celestial body, must prevail in all worlds. Presently, Odin's great palace came into view. It was Snorri's first sight of it from the outside for, on the previous day when he had ridden from it with Wulfhere to Valhalla, he had been so excited that he had not looked back. Now he beheld it in its breathtaking beauty. Unlike the other halls he had seen, which had been of more traditional construction that might be described as '13$^{th}$ Century vernacular', this one was built entirely of dressed stone and was quite vast in its proportions. It had many doorways and large, glazed windows, and clearly had three separate floors. The roof was covered by dark grey slates and, beneath the eaves, the top of the wall was decorated by a long frieze depicting scenes of conflict and accomplishment. At the ground floor, the entrances were surrounded by stone pillars and porticos, the latter decorated with gilded images of fantastic beasts, warriors, smiths, and vegetable tracery. Snorri reined in his horse, lost in wonder.
"Impressive, isn't it?", said Shiner as Galdrafaxi also drew to a halt. "Wulfhere told me that he had made changes. No more wooden walls or oak shingles on the roof. No more rushes on the floor, but marble slabs. You and I were away for an awful long time. I like the chimneys, though. My wife had one installed, as you saw, and they draw away the smoke. Wulfhere says the style developed over the hundreds of years that we were absent, and is influenced lately by Italian tastes."

"It is indeed beautiful", Snorri admitted, but tell me, what other advances have been made? I see the warriors – apart from those in Valhalla – armed with those bang-sticks, but have they, for instance, found a cure for the tooth-ache? Not long before I died, I had a terrible tooth-ache and had to have the offending tooth drawn. It was very painful."

Shiner laughed.

"Snorri, you are looking at fashions, not at the reality of Asgard. Look, if you like, at the reality that lies underneath the illusion – it can do no harm here, and I know you are capable of it – but here there is no tooth-ache or sickness. Was I not healed fully, after being recently restored from death?"

Snorri considered opening his vision to encompass the reality below. He knew that, as Shiner said, he could have done it, but he was afraid of disappointment. In encountering the terrifying, raw forces of fire and ice, he had seen enough reality for an entire series of lifetimes. He would settle for the illusion for now. Whatever illusion was involved in the path they rode, it seemed pretty convincing; the chalky, rutted country path that they had followed from Shiner's hall gave way to a firmer surface covered by crushed stone, which terminated at the expansive, slabbed forecourt of the palace. The horses' hooves clopped noisily across the flags as they approached the low balustrade and the stone steps that rose towards the main entrance. Grooms were approaching at a trot to take the reins of their horses, but were interrupted as Odin himself emerged from the doorway, walking quickly and followed at a respectful distance by two manservants.

"Stay in the saddle, boys!", he shouted, "we have much to see today, and I know you have already enjoyed a good breakfast!"

To Snorri's right, a raven croaked its agreement, and he marvelled that he had not noticed the bird before. In an uncharacteristically plebeian gesture, Odin put two fingers to his mouth and emitted a high, piercing whistle. In response came a rush of wind, stirring up dust from the forecourt and forcing all of them – except for Odin – to shield their eyes. When they looked again, an enormous, black stallion stood beside Odin, nuzzling at his pocket for a treat.

Allfather reached into one of his capacious pockets, brought out a sugar lump, and held it to the stallion's lips with palm extended. It was gratefully received by the horse as Snorri rubbed his eyes. It was hard to focus on the magnificent steed. Like Shiner's Galdrafaxi, it embodied the very essence of equine perfection, but to an even greater degree. Its proportions were perfect, but they seemed to flash and change as though it occupied several dimensions at once. At one moment it appeared a quite ordinary black stallion, if unusually large; the next moment, it had eight legs, and the attachment of the additional four legs was entirely feasible and normal, as though all horses should be built that way. Despite his earlier commitment not to look beyond illusion, Snorri was overcome by the temptation and opened his inner eye a little. He shuddered and stiffened in horror as the eight-legged horse resolved itself into a gigantic spider. Beneath the image, Snorri sensed, there was a still deeper layer containing something primaeval and horrific. To the left of the spider, a large, pulsing eye suddenly became manifest, and he was forced to shut down the vision, only to find himself looking into Odin's single eye.

"Thank you, Master Snorri", Odin said in a deep and laconic tone, "I think you have seen quite enough. This is Sleipnir, the only horse that will ever do for me."

Snorri blushed in embarrassment that his prying had been so easily detected, but Odin made no more of it. Instead, he mounted Sleipnir and, dismissing the herald, bade Shiner and Snorri follow him. They rode for about half a mile towards the hill's summit, which was crowned by a conical, flat-topped, grassy mound. On top of the mound, under an ornate canopy, was a golden throne guarded by two armed men. The trio dismounted and, with Odin in the lead, they ascended a steep flight of steps that rose straight to the top. When they were about half-way up, the guards sprang to attention and then levelled their spears in a fighting pose.

"Who approaches Allfather's throne?", one of them challenged in a loud voice.

"Allfather himself", replied Odin, "stand down, chaps."

The warriors relaxed and assumed the 'at ease' posture, still alert. The trio completed the ascent and at last stood upon the small plateau, next to the throne. Snorri could not help noticing that both the guards were blind, their eye sockets covered by closed lids with nothing behind. One had a long, horizontal scar that ran across both eyes and the bridge of the nose.

"This", Odin announced grandly with arms spread, "is Hliðskjálf, my high throne from which I can see into all the worlds. None may sit upon it but Frigg, my wife, and myself. As you can see, it is guarded by blind warriors who can be trusted not to abuse their position. But make no mistake, their hearing is excellent. They were trained by Heimdall, who you will meet later. Skírnir, punch one of them. Your choice which one."

Walking as lightly as he could (which meant as quietly as a cat) and holding his breath, Shiner approached the right-hand warrior and threw a punch directed straight at his nose. His fist met hide-covered wood with a resounding thump as the guard instantly raised his shield, and Shiner drew back nursing his bruised fist.

"Now, you two, the other man with me is called Snorri Sturluson. Threaten him, but do not hurt him."

No sooner had Odin spoken, but Snorri felt one spear-point touching his solar plexus, while another tickled his spine between the shoulder blades. He breathed very carefully, and Allfather laughed.

"See what I mean? The perfect guards! Recruited from Einherjar whose last mortal wounds left them blind. Anyway, I just thought you might like to see it. On to our next destination!"

A question had been forming in Snorri's mind, something that had always exercised his curiosity.

"My Lord", he asked hesitantly, "the lore tells us that Freyr once dared to sit upon your high throne. Was he punished for that?"

Odin's one eye opened wide, and his lips curled back in a wolfish grin.

"Punished? Ha! I should say he was punished! But I didn't have a hand in it. The silly boy fell in love with that Etin lass, what was her name? Gerd, that was it. He married her, and she made his life a

misery. Always complaining that it was too warm here in Asgard, and that she was no happier in Light-Elf-Home, which is Freyr's domain. What's more, he had to stop chasing tail, which was his favourite occupation. He's not depicted as a phallic God for nothing. He tried being a battle-God, and a God of farming, but at the end of the day she was always on to him, slyly asking whether he'd met any women and then accusing him of being unfaithful whether he had or he hadn't. Anyway, she got on well enough with Freyr's step-mother, Skadi. Both Etins, you see? And now they both spend most of their time at some skiing resort in the mountains of Etin-Home, so Freyr is free again to chase as much tail as he likes in Midgard. The whole affair cost me an arm and a leg, though, didn't it Skírnir?"
"Yes, my Lord", Shiner replied sheepishly.
Odin surveyed the expanse of scenery below them with satisfaction, deeply inhaling the clean air.
"Well, we can't spend all day up here", he exclaimed jovially. "It's getting on for noon, and Bifröst should look stunning at this time of day."
He started back down the steps again, humming a cheerful ditty, and Shiner followed close behind. Snorri moved to follow them, but a guard caught his sleeve.
"Begging your pardon, Sir", he said, "but it's an honour to meet you. No offence meant, sticking my spear against your ribs like that, but orders is orders. May I touch your face?"
Snorri stood still as the guard's questing fingers rapidly explored his face. The guard smiled.
"It's a nice face, Sir. Kindly. Your reputation goes before you, and it will go still further. We blind ones sometimes see further than sighted folk can."
Snorri looked at the ravaged face and muttered his thanks, aware of Odin's footsteps retreating down the mound.
"In your own time, Master Snorri!"
It was a reprimand, and Snorri hurried after Shiner and Odin, scurrying down the steps as fast as he could without breaking his

neck. At the foot of the mound, they found their mounts waiting for them, grazing on the thick grass.

From Hliðskjálf, they travelled downhill at a fast trot that Snorri found tiring. Odin repeatedly looked up at the sun, tracking her progress across the sky. Eventually, he looked back over his shoulder.
"I fear we must canter, gentlemen, otherwise we shall miss the event", he declared.
Shiner nodded, and suddenly Snorri found himself quite alone. The other two had simply disappeared. He reined in his piebald, looking all around to see where they had gone, but saw nothing but fields, trees, becks and a lonely lark that sang in the sky. Then, as quickly as he had disappeared, Shiner stood next to him again.
"Sorry, Snorri", he said. "When Odin says 'a canter' he means something close to the speed at which you and I travelled between the Nine Worlds. Galdrafaxi could keep up, but we both forgot that you have an ordinary mount. Leave Betsy here and climb up behind me."
Snorri dismounted and sprang up onto Galdrafaxi's back, marvelling again at the new vigour that coursed through him. Shiner whispered a few words into the piebald's ear, and then they departed. In a second, Galdrafaxi and his riders halted next to Sleipnir. Odin, who had already dismounted and had been contemplating the changed scenery, turned to greet them.
"You took your time", he grumbled.
Having only just recovered from the rapid displacement, Snorri now also surveyed the scene, and felt giddy. His knees buckled, and he snatched at Shiner's arm for support. They stood at the edge of a vast, round void into which every river and stream of Asgard debouched, pouring over the edge and joining to form a near-continuous, circular waterfall. The centre of the void was inky-black except where illuminated by stars and nebulae.
"Should be noon about… now", said Odin, and looked skyward. Sunna, at the very apex of her day's travel, was hidden behind a passing cloud. In irritation, he snapped his fingers and the offending

cloud dissolved as though it had never existed. Bright sunlight flooded the vista before them, to be broken into a trillion fragments as it met the cascading drops of water. The result was a rainbow such as Snorri had never seen, nor could have imagined. Great bands of every colour coalesced, dispersed, and coalesced again in a constantly shifting display, creating a brilliant, opalescent rainbow cloud. Odin grunted in satisfaction.

"I knew you would like to see this, Snorri. I never grow tired of seeing it, and come every other day to watch it. You call it Bifröst, the rainbow bridge, though it is not in truth a bridge, for it only looks like this at the point where the five heavenly roads enter Asgard, and only once per day. Still, it is a beautiful sight, is it not? I can't even claim credit for it; it just happened."

He turned to look at Snorri, and it seemed to Snorri that the face had changed. The grimness and the deep wrinkles of experience had dropped away, revealing a countenance of youthful innocence suffused with joy.

"You know what?", Odin continued, "I like best the things the things that I didn't create, build, or put into order. They always contain the loveliest surprises, and even when the surprise is strange or dark, it becomes a challenge, something to rectify or accommodate. That's why I like you humans. You are so unpredictable. Sometimes you present me with small, wonderful things, like a little girl offering me a card that she has made using paints and flowers. At other times, you generate horrors of a kind that I could not have dreamt up myself. I can put up with the blackness, and show you the way out, but you will have to learn for yourselves how to deal with the greyness that is coming."

Snorri was confused, and was about to say so, when the sun passed her zenith and was masked by another cloud. The opalescent vision disappeared, and Odin was again the grim, wolfish God that Snorri had previously known.

Betsy, the piebald, came galloping down from the higher ground, slowed to a trot, and approached Snorri, flanks heaving. She looked proud of herself that she had managed to catch up with the swifter, magical horses, and she nuzzled at his pocket for a reward. He stroked her head and neck.

"I'm sorry, Betsy, but I have nothing to give you", he said, "though you have done very well."

Shiner leaned towards his ear.

"Just wish it, my friend. You still have some of your power, even here. Change the Narrative, as you put it yourself."

Snorri looked at him and understood. He reached into his left-hand pocket and discovered a half-dozen of brown sugar lumps. Taking two of them, he held them before Betsy's nose and was rewarded by the gentle touch of her broad teeth and moist tongue on his palm as she took them. Odin was already in the saddle.

"Off again, boys", he said. "Away to Himinbjörg. It's not far this time, so try to keep up!"

At Himinbjörg, the gatehouse dwelling of the guardian-God Heimdall, there was excitement. Valkyries had just arrived, bearing two recently-deceased warriors. The latter had not yet regained consciousness, and lay on straw-filled pallets. Both wore bloodstained uniforms of blue, with yellow collars and cuffs. One bore a single puncture wound, a simple slit above the heart; the other had a gaping hole in his chest. Heimdall looked up as Odin, Shiner and Snorri entered.

"Two new acquisitions for Valhalla, Allfather", he said, "the first in a very long time."

Odin regarded them with satisfaction.

"Yes, I have had my eye on these two for some time. A war has broken out in Midgard between the Swedes and the Rus. These brothers are Swedish, and they come from an old, rural family that secretly honours the old ways. Not many of those around these days. Let them sleep for now, I shall revive and mend them later. Right now, I want you to meet our guest, Snorri Sturluson. Snorri, meet your ancestor."

Heimdall beamed a smile as he extended his right hand, and Snorri was gratified to see that he really did have golden teeth. He was dressed entirely in white, and had that inner luminescence that

Snorri had seen before in divine beings. His clothes were of the same, modern cut as Odin's, but suspended from a chain around the neck was a golden gorget, on which the image of a ram's head was embossed. The face and eyes, however, entranced Snorri the most: the face was long and somewhat ovine, and the brown eyes were wide-set and had horizontal pupils like those of a sheep. He also lacked one ear. Heimdall laughed warmly as he shook Snorri's hand and noted his astonished gaze.

"I have two ears, grandson", he said, "but one resides in Mimir's Well along with Allfather's eye. That is how I am able to hear everything that goes on in the Nine Worlds."

Snorri smiled with delight to be thus addressed as 'grandson'. Well he knew the old story, in which Heimdall, in the guise of Rig, had descended among humankind and had mated with the three classes – thralls, yeomen and jarls – to sow the seed of divinity in them. Lovingly, he met the gaze of those strange eyes, and felt the love returned.

"Tell me", Heimdall continued, have you remembered the rune-lore that I taught? Do you use it? Does it prosper still?"

At first, Snorri felt like hanging his head in shame, but decided that it was not his fault that the inheritance had been squandered. His gaze still firm, he replied honestly.

"No, grandfather, I am sorry to say that the lore is fast fading from the memory of Men. I know a little of it, but it has been largely expunged by the interlopers, the Christians. At least, that is how it was when death called me away from Midgard; I cannot speak of the situation now. So many years have passed. If it is any consolation, Shiner – I mean Skírnir – has been teaching me, and thinks I may have some talent in that direction."

Heimdall gave a small, resigned nod.

"It is to be hoped that future generations will rediscover it. It was my tooth-gift to all my children, and their children and grandchildren."

Snorri would dearly have loved to pose many questions, but Odin was already thanking Heimdall for his time and hurrying Snorri to the door.
"So little time, and so much to see!", he boomed, and within a minute the trio had remounted and were trotting along another path.

The path led up from the gatehouse for a few miles, then down again into a deep, shadowy vale. Surrounding hills cut out all direct sunlight, and the moist ground became soft under the horses' hoofs. Soon they arrived at a dark pool surrounded by ancient alders and willows. A voice like the crackling of dry parchment addressed them from the cleft of a willow with twin trunks.
"Is that you, you old rogue?", it rasped. "And who are the two riders with you?"
Odin quickly slid from Sleipnir's saddle and strode towards the bifurcated willow. Snorri hastily followed, eager to see the next mystery revealed. Odin stood before a mummified head that rested in the cleft, stroking it gently.
"Hello, old friend, he said. "I'm sorry that I have not visited for a while. I have brought someone to see you."
The head wheezed a derisive laugh. Though mummified, the lips and the shrivelled eyes moved.
"Don't 'old friend' me, you plotting trickster", it whispered. "I see now whom you have brought. Stand aside so that I can see Snorri properly."
Odin moved to one side, and the head continued.
"I see you, Snorri, son of Sturla. I am Mimir, the ancient and wise. I foresaw your coming, as I foresee everything and know all that has passed, though I have to admit that I lost you for a while when you were in Niflheim. Never mind... I see your mind, and know it now. You did well. Better than I would have expected from a philandering skald who meddled too much in politics and paid the price."
Again, the wheezing laugh.
"But don't let me detain you", Mimir went on, "go and take your dip in my well. After all, that is why Odin brought you here, and it's not

as if I can prevent you. Just do not drink, or it will be the worse for you."

Snorri did not know what to say. Mimir's words left him feeling stripped naked, all masking pretences torn away. A philandering skald who meddled too much in politics and paid the price? Was that how he would be remembered? He turned silently to Odin, looking for reassurance, and Odin clapped him on the shoulder, his single blue-grey eye twinkling.

"Do not worry, dear Snorri", he said. "He has a disconcerting way of identifying our vulnerabilities and exposing them. Personally, I find that useful. Flattery makes a God – or a man – weak and foolish. Honest rede-men are to be treasured, even when the rede is hard to hear. But he is right: you and I must take a dip in his mere so that I can show you the nature of it. Remember what Mimir said, though; do not drink, not even a sip."

Snorri made to take off his boots, but Odin stopped him, took his arm, and hastened him to the well's edge.

"Just follow me", he commanded. "Breathe normally. This is no common water."

And with that, he waded into the mere, and Snorri followed. The bank shelved off rapidly, and Snorri quickly found himself out of his depth. He floundered, arms splashing, trying to keep his chin out of the water. Odin's previously submerged head reappeared. He rolled his eye.

"I should have anticipated this", he sighed, and placed both hands forcefully on Snorri's head, pressing him below the surface. He waited until the frantic struggling ceased, then sank again to confront his astounded but relieved companion.

"There", he said, looking into Snorri's frightened, staring eyes, "did I not tell you that this is no common water?"

Snorri looked to left and right, up and down. He found that he could indeed breathe as easily as if he were on dry land. Nor was his vision blurred; everything about him, including Odin's face, was crystal-clear. There was only a sense of weightlessness.

"Follow", commanded Odin again, and together they descended deeper into the pool. Daylight was replaced by an eldritch luminosity, and Snorri perceived that he stood at the centre of a vast hall that extended around him and above him. The hemispherical boundary was segmented into countless chambers, and a constant whispering from each of them assaulted his ears, merging and overlapping. Each chamber emitted its individual light, alternately shining and fading in different colours, and all of them seemed to be communicating something.

"You stand in the biggest library in the world", announced Odin. "Nay, in the multiverse. Here, in Mimir's Well, are all memories housed. I have one to add. Do you remember seeing it before? Let's see if we can find a place for it. Ah... here's an empty space!"

He put a hand into his capacious pocket, brought out several cylindrical vials, and unplugged them. Glowing, multi-coloured skeins of threads emerged and swam, as if by instinct, gratefully towards the cavity that Odin had selected. For Snorri, there was something fatefully familiar about them.

"You remember them, don't you?", said Odin with a smile. "The memories that you saw extracted from the dead woman who was being dismantled in Svartálfheim. I kept them for you, for more than four hundred years, so that you can see what happens. She will have been reincarnated many times now without them; it matters not to me. Now, in her present incarnation, she may suddenly have dreams of a past life. It was not an exciting one, so they should not distress her too much."

As Snorri watched, the threads seemed to take root and extend, reaching out to neighbouring cells and linking to them. They seemed to be searching for meaning, and he was about to comment on this when Odin plucked at his sleeve and led him downward towards two small pillars that rested on the bed of the mere. On one pillar rested an eye. It never blinked, for it had no lids, but was nevertheless in constant motion, surveying all the various pockets of the vast library and the interactions between them.

"My other eye, my left eye", said Odin. "The eye which Mimir vindictively extracted from me as the price for a sup of wisdom from his well. I got much the better of the bargain. I have my ravens, Huginn and Muninn of course, and they bring me information daily, but this is by far my greatest asset. It rests here forever. It reads the memories, and the memories weave into what is now and what is to come. From here, I read the past, the present and the future. The future, of course, has an element of unpredictability – mainly due to the capriciousness of you bloody mortals – but I foresee it surely most of the time. It took me a long time to learn to read the threads and their movements."

He gestured towards the other pillar, on which an ear rested. "Heimdall's ear. He made a similar bargain, sacrificing an ear. Now he hears everything that transpires in the Nine Worlds… well, most of them, anyway. We both lost sight and sound of you when you visited Muspelsheim and Niflheim."

Snorri could only gaze in wonder at the mystery that had been revealed to him. Standing there in this hall of records, he also began to connect with the whispering, the blinking lights, and the connecting threads. He saw wars, natural disasters and nations on the move, together with the petty preoccupations of millions of individuals and, not for the first time, felt totally overwhelmed. His knees buckled and his breath nearly stopped at the information overload. He felt as though his brain was about to burst out of his ears, and the next thing he knew was that Odin was dragging him by the collar across the sandy shore that encircled Mimir's Well. Lying on his back, Snorri patted his clothes and found they were not even damp. A shadow fell over him, and he looked up to see Shiner's concerned face.

"Are you alright?", Shiner asked. "What was it like down there?"
Snorri closed his eyes again for a moment, seeking to bring his thoughts back into some kind of normal order.

"It was like seeing everything at once", he gasped. "Everything. All that has been, and is, and may come to pass. It was too much for me, and I hope never to repeat the experience. For all that we have been through together, I am still but a man, and there is only so much that the mind can take."

Shiner looked away to where Odin was speaking to Mimir's head, the exchange of words too subdued to be heard.

"That was an overly large gift", he muttered quietly. "He never gave such a gift to anyone else, as far as I know. I wonder what the old trickster will want in return. A gift demands a gift."

If Odin heard anything of their conversation, he did not show it as he returned to them in his customary ebullient mood.

"Come on, Master Snorri", he boomed. "Don't lie there all day like a stranded fish! The day is drawing to a close, and you are both invited to take supper with me this evening. Now, say goodbye to Mimir, and let us be on our way."

Snorri and Shiner approached Mimir, who was dozing, eyes closed, in his willow-cleft. They both thanked him for his time. In reply, Mimir yawned and told them to fuck off.


As Sunna's two horses, Early-waker and All-swift, smelled the stable and completed their last leg towards the horizon, Odin, Shiner and Snorri likewise rode at an easy pace towards Odin's palace, alternating between a trot and a canter. A question occurred to Snorri.

"My Lord", he asked Odin, "there is something that puzzles me. I always thought that Mimir's well resided at the roots of Yggdrasil, but we have just visited it here in Asgard. How can that be?"

Odin looked at him with an expression of amused astonishment.

"At the roots of the World Tree?", he replied. "What a ridiculous idea! Is that what you wrote in your books? That would never do! I visit Mimir often to partake of his wisdom, old curmudgeon though he is. Imagine if I had to ride the length and breadth of the Tree every time I needed to talk to him. Preposterous!"

And with that, he cantered ahead. Snorri turned to Shiner, who shrugged.

"I am certainly learning a lot", said Snorri."

"And that, after all, is the whole purpose of your travels", Shiner replied with a smile.

# Chapter 14 - Explanations

Four hours later, after a sumptuous dinner in Odin's private chamber, the three of them relaxed in front of the hearth and sipped their brandy appreciatively.
"Well, Snorri", said Odin, putting his glass down, "have you enjoyed your visit to Asgard? I trust it has been educational?"
"It has been most educational, my Lord", Snorri replied. He hesitated before asking the obvious question.
"May I take it, then, that my visit is about to end?"
The single, twinkling eye held his gaze as Odin took another sip of brandy.
"Indeed it is", he replied evenly. "There has not been time to show you everything, but you have seen enough. Moreover, I don't want you to get too comfortable here, for your travels are not quite ended. Tomorrow, I want Shiner to take you to Jötunheim – Etin-home – so that you can make acquaintance with the Giants."
He saw Snorri's apprehensive expression, and continued.
"Now, now, there is no need to be afraid. They are a decent lot really, if somewhat uncouth. My mother's side of the family, you know. We quarrel, now and again, and thereby provide a lot of material for you earthly scribes and poets but, when all is said and done, we don't really hate each other. My son Thor has to go and beat them up, teach them a lesson now and again – but on the whole I regard them as a gentleman might regard his bucolic cousins."
Snorri swirled his brandy, deep in thought, while Odin and Shiner lit pipes of tobacco. What an adventure it had been! Sometimes it felt like only yesterday that the swords had ended his earthly life; at other moments, he could well believe that he had been on the road for over four hundred years. He had seen so much, and yet there was still no explanation. Looking up, he saw that Shiner was regarding him intensely as he puffed on his pipe, willing him to ask the question that was uppermost in both their minds. He tried to find diplomatic words, but there were none for such an occasion. He looked directly at Odin.

"Why, my Lord? Why this long journey? Why did you choose me to make it, and trouble Shiner so much to guide me? I own that I have learned more than any mortal might know, but what has been the point of it?"

Shiner re-lit his pipe from a taper, then spoke up in support of Snorri, abandoning his usual deferential attitude.

"Yes, Allfather, I would also like to know why you sent me to guide our friend to regions unknown even to you. And thereby brought us into perils leading almost to the extinction of my existence."

As if to emphasise the point, he blew at the flame and extinguished it. For the first time, Odin seemed discomfited. He laid down his pipe, brushed ash from his thighs, and took a sip of brandy. Then he shrugged, gave a brief, apologetic smile, and for once his gaze was not steady.

"Well…", he began, "look… you were never in that much danger, Shiner. It was a lot to ask, I admit, but I consulted the runes beforehand. I could not foresee all the details, but I knew that you would, eh, muddle through somehow… hmmm?"

Shiner smoked his pipe and held Odin's eye.

"It rather seems to me", he replied, "that it was Snorri who 'muddled through somehow'. I died. No, worse than died: my soul was drawn from me, and held captive by Jökulheið. It was Snorri who retrieved it, learned the magic so quickly, and brought me back here to be fully restored. He is a remarkable man, and I think you owe him – and me – a full explanation of what is going on here, and why you have put us through so much."

Odin tensed and, for an instant, his eye glowed red. He was not used to having his decisions questioned. Then, just as quickly, he recovered his composure. Raising his hands, palms outward, he resumed an attitude of charming affability.

"Gentlemen, gentlemen, let us not quarrel! It is true that I have put both of you to great trouble, but it has all ended well. And I had my motives. Deep motives."

He re-lit his pipe and leaned back in his armchair before continuing.

"In Midgard, things have not gone well for the Aesir over the past eight centuries. One after the other, traitor kings sold out to the

Christians – mainly for reasons of status, trade and politics – and forced their people to convert to the new religion. Wretches! Hounds have more loyalty! By your time in Midgard, Snorri, even Iceland had been Christian for two hundred years, as well you know. I tried to negotiate with Yahweh, but he sat in his wooden box and uttered not one word in reply. The White-Christ and his followers refuse even to recognise our existence, or call us demons as though we were mere mountain-trolls. Some simple folk in secluded valleys still honour us, away from the eyes and ears of the canting priests – you saw those two Swedish boys that my Valkyries brought in this afternoon – but they are very few. In England, Scotland and Vinland, small numbers still worship us at night, almost without knowing they do. They call me 'Old Nick', and think they honour the Christian devil. To be honest, it is embarrassing to have to take such petty crumbs of belief."

He paused to take a sip of brandy, and Snorri uncomfortably reflected that he, too, had been guilty of rejecting the Aesir until his post mortem adventures had exuberantly confirmed the error of his ways.

"You see", Odin went on, "belief is meat and drink to the gods. Every thought – even the negative ones – and every offering filters up to us and maintains our substance. After the prophecy of the Seeress, I feared Ragnarök but also looked forward to it in a way. It would have been such a glorious ending! And because Men knew it would bring their demise too, they tried to strengthen us, and crowded to join the Chosen, the Einherjar, who would fight with us in the final battle."

He shook his head sadly.

"But nothing is so destructive as being ignored. I have seen bone-yards full of dead gods who were abandoned by their people thousands of years ago, their very names forgotten. And that is where you come in, Snorri."

Snorri started at the mention of his name. He had been plunged into sadness at the thought of so much loss. He raised his head, stared at Odin, then at Shiner, and then back to Odin again.

"I? How do I come into it? I was a simple skald, and a Christian back then. I probably only made things worse."
Odin let out a loud guffaw of laughter, and Shiner gave a wry smile, "Oh, what a modest man you are! On your recent journey, you learned magic as though you were born to it, you saved Shiner, and made no boast of it, but even before you died you forged an even greater deed than that!"
Snorri thought hard, but could not imagine what Odin was driving at. He shook his head to show his incomprehension.
"You, Snorri Sturluson", said Odin, leaning towards him, "committed the names and deeds of the Aesir to writing more than any other. Sure, there are other fragments here and there… a mention from some bishop, an old law, a folk-belief… but no-one went as far as you did to preserve us in script. Script is powerful, as the Christians well know; it can communicate ideas across continents and across the years. As long as the book remains intact, and is read, the names and deeds live on. That was your gift to us. And you did it joyfully, without blaming or denigrating us. Among the English, the Franks, the Alemanni and the Lombards there is barely a mention of us. Only in the northlands did the knowledge survive, and for that I thank you on behalf of all the Aesir."
Snorri was astounded. He blinked hard at this revelation, and took a large gulp of brandy, which made him cough.
"I… I am pleased to have been of service, my Lord", he stuttered, "but that still does not tell us why it was so important to send us on our perilous journey, or why we must still visit the Etins in their abode."
Shiner nodded in agreement.
"Be patient; I was getting to that", Odin replied. "By my reading of the runes, and all the indications from Mimir's Well, all is not yet lost. There will come a revival, though we may have to wait a while, perhaps a couple of centuries. When it comes, at the crucial point, I want someone there in the thick of it to convey the absolute truth – no holds barred – with conviction. As the Christians would term it, a messiah. And I don't care whether we Aesir come over as less than perfect, as long as people believe. That is why I took pains to ensure

you survived the dying process with all your faculties, and why I sent Shiner to take you on that remarkable journey. You were the perfect candidate. You had to see everything, even the dangerous parts, and understand it all, so that you can go back to Midgard and be my prophet."

Odin looked piercingly at Snorri, unblinking, challenging him to object, but Snorri´s head was spinning and he could formulate no answer. It was Shiner who, puffing on his pipe and appearing relaxed, spoke next.

"That´s a shame. I had hoped to gain a companion on the many missions you and the others impose on me. It´s a lonely business, you know. Snorri shows enormous promise, and is a natural in the magical arts. With some coaching he could become my equal and halve the burden."

He leaned down and flicked some imaginary dust from his right boot.

"Except, knowing you and the other Aesir – and Vanir – you would simply find twice as many missions to accomplish, and send each of us out alone. No rest for the wicked, eh?"

For several seconds, Odin continued to gaze at Snorri as if he had not heard Shiner, but then he dragged his gaze slowly away, still unblinking, to regard Shiner.

"Oh, don't worry, Master Skírnir", he said in a low voice. "When the time comes, you will be going with him."

Odin stood and, as if on cue, a footman opened the door of the chamber. It was clear that the audience was at an end. Snorri and Shiner also rose from their chairs, bowed, and made to leave.

"Get a good night's sleep, lads", said Odin, "you have a long journey ahead of you tomorrow."

Snorri was already outside when Odin called Shiner back and bade him close the door. Snorri shrugged and started back towards his apartment. Inside the chamber, Odin briefly addressed Shiner.

"Skírnir, there is something I want you to take with you. A mere trifle, a gift to mollify the Etins. Some herbs that one of their shamans asked me for."

He reached into an inside pocket and brought out a tightly bound package with an oilskin covering. Shiner took it, bowed, and left. Hurrying, he quickly caught up with Snorri.

"Snorri, my friend, I mean to spend tonight at home with my wife. I see her little enough as it is. Will you be our guest again? Galdrafaxi can have us there in the blink of an eye."

Snorri smiled broadly, agreed immediately, and went to get his meagre possessions from his room. On the way to the stable, Shiner spoke again.

"Not a word to Gróa about tonight's business, eh? She worries a lot. I might have known that the Old Man had something ambitious in mind; he does nothing without reason. But be careful, Snorri. You and I are but pawns, and he expends those without hesitation if it suits the bigger plan. Whatever happens, know that I will be looking out for you."

Standing at Galdrafaxi's side, he extended his hand, and Snorri shook it warmly. Then they mounted and, as Shiner had promised, were at his steading in the blink of an eye.

At first light, the pair stood before Shiner's verandah, and Gróa hugged both of them in farewell. Galdrafaxi was already saddled, and seemed not to object to the extra saddle-bag that contained Snorri's spare clothes, pipe, tobacco, and the bottle of brandy that he had filched from his room. With a wave to Gróa and the servants, they were soon on their way, trotting down the narrow, sandy path that led to the gate of Asgard. The grey light of dawn gave way to a golden glow as Sunna's wain approached the rim, and birdsong reached a crescendo. Shiner turned in the saddle to face Snorri.

"Beautiful, isn't it? I always love this time of day, whether in Asgard, Midgard or Vanaheim. You only get it in those three worlds. That's why we are taking this part at the easy trot of a normal horse; we can always pick up the pace later, once we are on the main road."

He sighed as he surveyed the peach-coloured sunrise with satisfaction, inhaling the clean, cool air of morning.

"I could wish that Allfather and the rest of them would cut me some slack, so that I could experience this more often, and the other small pleasures of a peaceful life."

Snorri's finely tuned ear caught the condition in the sentence.

"But?", he said simply, and Shiner laughed.

"Yes, my friend, 'but'. I chose this life, this eternal life. When I was an earthly magician, so long ago now, I worked hard to master the skills so that I would be able to shape things according to my will, eliminating every challenge and obstacle. I nearly succeeded, for there were none who could stand against me in the end. The only things I had to fear were old age and death, and those came around with tedious regularity. I advised kings and emperors, worked spells on their behalf, and saw all of them fall victim to their own folly. Or old age, in rare cases. When last I died, I was tired of living and desired only the cessation of existence, but Odin rescued me. He gave me new adventures and purpose, even though I don't understand the nature of the game half the time. And when I am on leave, here in Asgard, I appreciate the small, free pleasures that cannot be bought with wealth or power. It is in the narrow space between hardships and those pleasures that true life is to be found. If more people in Midgard were to appreciate that, there would be less strife, don't you think?"

Snorri nodded. He remembered, among his own last words, 'Út vil ek' – 'I want out' - indicating his desire to retreat from the high politics of Norwegian kings and resume the quiet life. Nevertheless, the politics had followed and slain him.

Now, as Sunna's shining wain emerged over the rim of Asgard, casting light all about, they approached the gaping circle that marked Asgard's gate. The first rays brilliantly illuminated the trees, grass and heather, making the dew on them to shine as diamonds, but the void was still in shadow. Of other life there was no sign. The sheep had ceased to bleat, and the cacophony of birdsong was stilled. No guard challenged them, and even Heimdall seemed to be asleep. It seemed as though Odin had ordained that their leaving should be noticed by none.

"Ready?", asked Shiner, and with that he spurred Galdrafaxi out into space and onto the road to Jötunheim.

# Chapter 15 – Jötunheim

Two days later, at the border of Etin-home, Galdrafaxi carried his two riders along a bare ridge at an ambling walk. The day was sunny, and Snorri's eyelids grew heavy, the pace gently rocking him asleep. The only thing keeping him awake was a pervasive odour of sweat whenever the breeze shifted to blow directly into his face. Puzzled, he raised each of his arms in turn and sniffed at his armpits. Sure, he smelt a bit rank – after all, they had been on the road for two days without any chance for a bath – but the odour was definitely not his own.
"Have you ever seen an Etin?", Shiner asked.
"Yes", Snorri replied. "I saw one in Vanaheim when I was gardening. Little creature, looked a lot like a mushroom. Why do you ask?"
"Because we are riding on one right now", said Shiner. "We're on his leg. I assume the lazy brute is supposed to be on guard here at the border, but decided to take a nap. I'll hail him when we reach his chest."
They crossed the giant's groin area, negotiating the thick folds of his breeches where they gathered at the crotch. A deep grunt came from up ahead, and an enormous hand rose into the air to cast a shadow over them. Fortunately, the motion was exceedingly slow, as if a passing cloud gradually eclipsed the sun. Shiner twitched his heels against Galdrafaxi's flanks, urging him to quicken the pace, and they were at the belt line before the hand landed to scratch at the crotch. As they crossed the belly, which heaved up and down like the tides of the ocean, a thought occurred to Snorri.
"I don't mean to be nuisance", he said, "after all, you're the one with all the experience of Etins, but, erm… might I point out that if you hail him from his chest, he might be surprised and sit bolt upright? Even if he does so slowly, we'll be on a vertical surface with a long drop below us. Just thought I'd mention it."
"Good point", Shiner replied, "perhaps it would be better to address him from the side of his head", and he steered Galdrafaxi to the right and towards the sleeping Etin's left shoulder. As he did so, the giant decided to roll over onto his left side, and they were

forced to make a gallop and then a flying leap in order to avoid being crushed. When they had recovered their breath, Shiner directed the horse to stand level with the closed eyes.

"Hello there!", he yelled. "Is this how you welcome visitors to Jötunheim?"

The giant's eyes half-opened, and closed again. The right hand swept the face, as though a fly had tickled the nose. Then the eyes opened fully and stared at them for a full ten seconds before the astonished giant hauled himself up to rest on one elbow, sending a shower of dust and rocks toward Snorri and Shiner. Galdrafaxi sidestepped neatly to avoid a sheep-sized boulder. Then came the giant's challenge as he sat up, a deep, thunderous rumble.

"FEE! Er, how's it go again? Oh yeah… FEE, FIE, FO, FUM!"

Shiner and Snorri simply sat, dumbfounded, in the saddle.

"What?", said Shiner.

"What d'you mean?", replied the sleepy Etin as he rubbed his eyes. Shiner looked up at the enormous face. Even sitting, the giant towered over them like a tall cliff.

"I mean, what's with the 'Fie, fo, fum' stuff? What does it mean?"

The giant simply stared back, clearly having trouble to get his brain into action. Eventually he spoke again.

"It's what we have to say these days. It's the fashion… some nonsense that came over from Midgard. Don't ask me what it means. Anyway, YOU may take it to mean 'who the heck are you, and why have you woken me up?'".

Shiner smiled.

"Do you not recognise me, Fornrugg? I know that it has been a long time since I was last here, but I still remember you."

The Etin stared hard at him, shrinking as he did so to about three times the height of a man, from 'gigantic' to merely 'huge'.

"Orvandil? Is it you?", he asked, and his face broke into a broad smile. "It *is* you!", he cried and, with a delighted whoop, picked Shiner up, tossed him in the air and caught him again. "We thought you were dead! There was word from the Thurses that you died in Niflheim."

Shiner laughed as he dangled in Fornrugg's grip.

"It would appear that the Norns have other plans for me. And now, please put me down again or you will worry my companion."
Fornrugg gently lowered Shiner to the ground. Squatting, he turned to face Snorri.
"Pleased to meet you. And what may your name be? Though any friend of Orvandil's is a friend of mine."
"Snorri Sturluson, at your service", said Snorri with a bow. "How did you do that just now? Getting so much smaller, I mean. It's a strange and wonderful ability."
"Never really thought about it", the Etin replied. "Get smaller, get bigger again; it's just something we can do. Might just as well ask yourself why you *can't* do it. Anyway, smaller's the fashion now, except when we're on guard duty We got a new boss, and he says we're not to go around intim… intimid… making people frightened any more."
Snorri looked Fornrugg up and down, taking in the full eighteen feet of his current stature.
"Well, you still look pretty awe-inspiring to me. Can you get smaller still? In Vanaheim, I saw an Etin who was tiny. Wearing his hat, I mistook him for a mushroom at first."
Again came the broad grin.
"Why, that could've been my little nephew, Ankle-biter! He's doing his apprenticeship over there! Seeing the worlds, he is. Was he pushing a wheelbarrow?"
Snorri nodded.
"Yeah, he says he doesn't like that work, but it won't be for long. He's a bright lad, and if he does alright in Vanaheim, he'll be off to Svartálfheim next to learn smithing, which will be more to his taste. He's clever; he can even write."
With a cough, Shiner interrupted the conversation.
"Speaking of writing", he said, bringing out a scroll, "we have a letter of introduction from Allfather himself. A passport, if you like. Would you like to see it?"
Fornrugg reached down and took the scroll, unfurled it, and with a creased brow made a show of inspecting its contents.

"I.. I… expect it will all be in order. Look, Orvandil, you know I can't read. You tried to teach me my Futhark years and years ago, and I've forgotten it all now. Tell you what, I'm not allowed to leave my post, but you just get on your way to the castle and I'll send a signal for someone to meet you halfway and guide you in."

He searched around among the rocks and mounds until he found a horn that was about six feet long and looked to be made of ivory. Putting it to his lips, he gave one long blast, followed by two shorter ones.

"One to get their attention" Fornrugg said, "two to tell 'em it's a friend coming."

They thanked Fornrugg and mounted again. Just as they were about to depart, the giant spoke to Shiner in the quietest voice that he could manage.

"You won't say anything about me being asleep on watch, will you? I like doing this duty. It's nice and peaceful, and hardly anyone comes here these days."

Shiner assured him that nothing would be said of it, and they went on their way.

The day was one of sunshine and broken cloud, though the wind was chilly; the kind of weather, Snorri reflected, that one might expect in early October. The landscape was rather barren, with sparse, thin grass and stunted birch trees striving for existence among rocky outcrops. It very much reminded him of his former home in Iceland. Yet, as they came over a ridge, they were confronted by a broad plain with fields of vegetable crops, and these were being harvested by small, distant figures. Approaching closer, their appearance became more discernible.

"Are those Vanir working in the fields?", Snorri asked.

"Yes", Shiner replied. "Another surprise for you?"

Snorri wondered what could ever tempt Vanir to practise agriculture in this barren land, instead of on the fertile soil of Vanaheim, and he asked Shiner whether they were perhaps thralls or hostages.

"Not at all", Shiner replied. "They are here entirely of their own free will, as part of the arrangement. You remember that the Vanir employ Etins to temper unruly growth, do the pruning and carry away detritus? Everything the Vanir touch turns to luxurious, excessive growth. Here it's the opposite. The Etins can't grow anything worth a damn; everything they touch withers or is stunted, but they still have to eat. So they work an exchange system, under which their youngsters are apprenticed for a while to labour in a world utterly different to their own. Some resent it and grumble, of course, but in adulthood they generally look back fondly on their apprenticeships."
Snorri nodded, understanding, and Shiner continued.
"The system also gives them valuable experience, fosters mutual understanding, and helps to prevent war."

A walled city with a towering citadel at its centre had come into view. Horns blew, and the main gate opened. Suddenly, a dozen truly gigantic Etins rushed out of the open portal and down the road towards them. They brandished stone axes that had entire tree trunks as their hafts, and they roared a murderous intent. Aghast, Snorri remembered a warding spell that he had read in Shiner's book, and he began to raise his arm to cast it while Galdrafaxi shifted uneasily beneath them. Shiner caught sight of the motion and caught Snorri's arm, forcing it down again.
"Just stand your ground!", he commanded.
Roaring again and again, the Etin warriors came on at a tremendous pace, their long, stocky legs quickly eating up the mile of distance until Snorri feared that the stone axes must fall upon them within a matter of seconds. Then, just thirty yards away, the giants halted, raised their arms with a final 'YAAAAH!', and burst into laughter.
"Bet that scared 'em!", shouted one as he slapped his thigh in mirth.
"Nah", replied another, "these tinies are tough ones. They usually run like the wind."
"Yeah, you got that right", added another. "Still, the one at the back's looking pretty pale. I wonder if he's shat himself?" And with

that, he knelt down, lowered his head until it was a few feet away from the saddle, and sniffed loudly. He stood again, disappointed. "You're right", he admitted, "not a whiff of it. He addressed himself directly to Shiner and Snorri.

"C'mon, you two, you must've been a bit frightened?"

Before either Shiner or Snorri could reply, the hubbub was checked, starting with the warriors furthest away from them. A much smaller Etin, only twenty feet tall, was pushing his way among them. He had a grey beard, and bore an elaborate staff of office.

"You young hooligans!", he shouted. "Have you forgotten the King's law? THOU SHALT NOT FRIGHTEN THE TINIES EXCEPT AT THE KING'S COMMAND! You should all be ashamed of yourselves."

The younger giants shuffled their feet and hung their heads. One began to diminish in size and kicked the foot of his nearest companion, who also shrank. Very soon, all the company had reduced their size to the smallest they could comfortably manage. The greybeard, satisfied that he had things under control, continued to berate them.

"I know all of your names and faces. Now, back to the city; I'll deal with you later. Except you, Gólandi; you can go and relieve Fornrugg and do a double watch."

With a deal of embarrassed muttering, most of the Etins plodded back to the city gate. The one named Gólandi headed down the road in the direction whence Snorri and Shiner had come. When a hundred yards away, he yelled 'YAAAH!' at a group of toiling Vanir, and they laughed and thumbed their noses in response.

The greybeard with the ornate staff hobbled up to Snorri and Shiner. He straightened his robe, which was patterned in orange, brown and black.

"My apologies for that lamentable display", he said. "Please understand that it was merely the ebullience of youth, and that the culprits will be duly punished. You are welcome here. I trust you have some letter..." Seeing Shiner's face properly for the first time, his face lit up.

"I was going to say 'of introduction', but you, my dear Orvandil, require no introduction. Why, it is good to see you again! It was rumoured that you were dead!"
Shiner smiled at his old friend.
"Langbard, it is good to see you too! Indeed, I was dead, but thereby hangs another tale. It was thanks to the mortal behind me that I live again. Let me introduce you to Snorri Sturluson."
Langbard bent down to peer at Snorri's face.
"Snorri, son of Sturla, you say?" He looked away and scratched his head. "I think I recall such a name... a human poet and teller of tales... didn't have much good to say about us, if I remember rightly. Is this him?"
In deference, Snorri dismounted and bowed to the Etin, who clearly held some high office.
"The same, Sire. I regret any offence I may have caused, back in the day. I only repeated old stories that I had heard, and I have had a great deal of education since. I have been sent here for the completion of that education."
Langbard was mollified but confused.
"But... but... that Snorri lived centuries ago. How can you be the same man? Humans are like mayflies, and rarely live beyond seventy years."
Snorri was about to reply when Shiner interrupted, smoothly presenting the scroll of introduction penned by Odin himself.
"It is a long story, Langbard, and you shall hear all of it in due course. In the meantime, let me present our references."
Langbard took the scroll and read some of it aloud.
"Let's see... 'We, Odin, Allfather, helmet-bearer, wide-in-wisdom etcetera, etcetera, do hereby request and require... safe passage... education in the history and ways of...'; yes, that all appears to be in order. Gentlemen, I apologise again for the delay and the insolent welcome. Please follow me."
He turned and shambled back towards the city. Shiner and Snorri followed on Galdrafaxi.

As he passed under the archway of the city's main gate, Snorri looked up in wonder at the architecture that surrounded him. It was, of course, of cyclopean proportions, though not quite as large as he had expected. The height of the gateway, for example, he estimated at about one hundred feet – far too low for the three-hundred-foot denizens that he had already encountered that day, unless they got down on their hands and knees. The main thing that struck him was the fineness of the stonework, which was precisely carved and faced, with barely a joint visible between the individual stones. He had expected something much cruder, but then reminded himself that Etins were master masons. Had not an Etin been employed by the Aesir to build the walls of Asgard, only to be tricked out of his wage by Loki's cunning? Emerging from the shadow of the gateway into bright sunshine again, Snorri became aware of the mood of excitement that surrounded him. There were no cheers, but there was a continuous hubbub and chatter of many bass and baritone voices, and the words that predominated were "Orvandil! Orvandil has returned!", and he felt a little envious of his friend's fame. With Langbard leading the way, they rode along a wide high street towards the citadel, the street's width somewhat constricted by the crowds of giants who lined the route. Looking up, he saw tall windows filled with curious faces and Etin-children being held up to get a better view. Eventually, at the termination of the street just in front of the citadel, a vast golden throne came into view, and in it sat a regal figure: the King of Jötunheim. Shiner reined Galdrafaxi to a halt, dismounted, and bade Snorri follow him on foot.

"Just walk beside me, and follow my lead in everything", he whispered.

Arriving at the plaza that lay in front of the throne, Shiner bowed deeply, and Snorri followed suit. As they held the bow, the surrounding hubbub was stilled until silence reigned and larks could be heard in the sky above. The silence was broken by a deep, melodious voice whose echoes rumbled along the streets, reaching every member of the expectant crowd.

"Orvandil Far-Traveller, what a great pleasure it is to see you here. Please stand straight, so that I can see your face better."
Snorri held his bow as Shiner straightened and returned the greeting.
"Your Majesty, I thank you. It is a pleasure to be here."
"And who is your companion?", the King enquired. "Is he also a far-traveller? I do not recognise him."
"Though you may not recognise his face, Sire", said Shiner, "I think you may have heard his name. This is Snorri, son of Sturla, who wrote a great deal about Etins and Gods a few centuries ago. He has done a great deal of travelling in the intervening years, so yes, he is a far-traveller."
The King turned towards a courtier who stood to his right behind the throne, and quietly asked a few questions. Satisfied by the answers, he nodded and addressed Snorri.
"Snorri Sturluson, please be upstanding. We have heard your name, and we have read your writings." He paused for a moment, then continued with a frown. "Are you here to mock us?"
Snorri was at first struck dumb, his mind frantically searching for reasons why the King of the Etins should think he had come to mock. Then he remembered his writings, in which he had often portrayed the Etins and Thurses as evil, brutish, hostile, and even cowardly. Gulping, he sought for an appropriate reply.
"Your Majesty", he said, "I certainly do not come to mock. It has already been pointed out to me that I made many errors in my works, in all respects. I come here to learn, that I may have an opportunity to correct those errors."
The King's stern features softened; he permitted himself a small, dignified smile, but it was in the eyes that warmth really showed.
"A good answer, Master Snorri. I can see that we shall have much to discuss."
Snorri relaxed, and allowed himself, for the first time, to fully take in the King's external aspects. He was certainly not ugly, by any measure. The face was daunting, but actually rather handsome in a harsh kind of way. The high forehead, deep brow, prominent cheekbones and strong jaw reminded him of a cliff-face carved by

time and weather. The hair and beard, greyed as if by the touch of hoar-frost, were neatly trimmed. On the shoulders rested a stole of ermine; below that a russet robe that extended to the knees, and below the robe's hem was fine hose of an ochre hue, terminating in black, polished shoes. In his right hand the King held a tall, darkly stained staff of wood – Snorri guessed that it was oak – on which twining serpents held a trail of runes worked in silver. The runes were angular like the Futhark, but the characters were different. In his left hand rested an orb inscribed with a snowflake symbol, which he recognised as the Hagall-rune. To the orb was added a flange bearing the Thurs-rune, and the point of that rune was directed inward towards the orb's centre. Snorri took it all in, speculated on the symbolism, but said nothing. His speculations were cut short as Shiner spoke up again.

"Sire, I bear a package that was entrusted to me by Odin himself. A quantity of herbs, he said, for one of your shamans. May I give it to you now?"

The King nodded, and the courtier stepped forward to accept the package. He immediately returned to his place and passed it on to a strangely-dressed figure who briefly emerged from the shadows behind. Snorri just had time to make out the bizarre garb: a ragged, antlered headdress with tassels that covered the eyes; a necklace made of horns, bones and skulls; and a cloak composed of the fur and feathers of many different beasts and birds. Bracelets made of bones and stones rattled as the creature moved, and then the creature was gone again. Snorri could only assume that this had been the shaman in question.

In the shady precincts of the citadel, the shaman Hrokkvir carefully opened the oilskin covering of the package. He was puzzled, because he had not requested any herbs from Odin. Perhaps another shaman had asked for them? There were other shamans among the Etins, it was true, but none held such high status as he did. Within the tightly bound pouch he found leaves, brown and desiccated, and he also found a letter addressed to him. It was written in Etin-runes, but the words made no sense at first reading.

Clearly, some kind of code had been employed, and he hurried to his chamber to decrypt it.

"Well," said the King, "I think a feast is in order to celebrate your visit. It will take some hours to prepare, so I will see to it that you are escorted to your quarters, where you can bathe, change, and take a light lunch." He rose, nodded, and made his way into the citadel. All others present bowed as he departed, and then another courtier approached Shiner and Snorri.
"If you would care to follow me, gentlemen?", he said, and led them into the interior.

Two adjacent rooms had hastily been prepared for them, and Snorri was surprised to see that all the furniture was of an appropriate size for human use, if rather on the large side. His bed was long and would easily have accommodated three people; his feet dangled above the floor as he sat on the edge of it, but it was soft and comfortable. Light entered via a high window, and a long, embroidered tapestry depicting creation scenes, the slaying of Ymir, and the struggles of Bergelmir and his family covered three of the four walls. As Snorri was surveying this, someone entered the room, and he was startled to see that it was a Wane, a male of the Vanir race. The Wane was close to Snorri's height – only an inch or two taller – and his delicate features were surmounted by a golden circlet that held his long, fair hair in check. He was carrying a wash basin, a pitcher of hot water, and a towel.
"Good afternoon, Sir", he said brightly, and proceeded to place the items on a dressing table. From a hidden pocket a comb, a razor, and a bar of soap were added to the array. The surprised Snorri finally managed to find words.
"You… you're a Wane!", he gasped.
"You are very observant, Sir", said the Wane smoothly. "Laukrún, at your service."
"I saw and heard that you chaps were here in Etin-home", said Snorri, confused, "but I thought you came here to work the fields."

"Indeed, Sir", agreed Laukrún, "I have had my share of planting and harvesting crops. Now I approach the end of my apprenticeship, and am given lighter and more agreeable duties. The Etins wisely deem it fitting and…" – he hesitated for a second – "more comforting for our smaller guests to be served by someone closer to their own size."
"Do you get many such guests?", Snorri asked.
"You and your friend are the first in about one hundred and fifty years", the Wane replied, "and the most honoured. Most are captives. The Etins still take human captives, very quietly and discreetly, when there are insufficient Vanir apprentices to deal with the farming. We, the more experienced Vanir, are put in charge of them. They are well treated, and quickly become quite pliable and obedient. Of course, they can never return to Midgard to tell their tales, which can be sad for the families they leave behind. For that reason, they – the Etins – prefer to take waifs and strays, abandoned children and the like. On the whole they work well, and it is a pity that we cannot get them to live longer. The last died a hundred years ago at the age of ninety."
Laukrún gave a slight bow and left the room, and Snorri stripped off his dusty clothes, washed, and shaved. Feeling refreshed, he noticed that clean clothes had been laid out on the bed. They were worn, but serviceable, and Snorri speculated that they were Laukrún's own. He felt glad that Odin had restored him to the body he had had in his early thirties, without the paunch he had acquired in later years.

As the last rays of the setting sun shone through the room's high window, a knock on the door woke Snorri from his nap.
"Come in", he said sleepily, and Shiner entered wearing a beaming smile. The smile was not all he wore: he was dressed in a bright-red tunic of decidedly ancient cut, completed by dark-green hose and an elaborately decorated leather belt.
"Look!", he exclaimed, "these are clothes that I left behind after my last visit! And still in perfect condition after… let's see… it must be

six hundred years ago. Well come on, Snorri, you can't lie there all evening; we have a feast to attend!"

Fifteen minutes later, they were seated at the King's high table in the great hall of the citadel. The King and Queen sat next to each other with Shiner and Snorri to either side of them, Snorri at the King's left hand and Shiner at the Queen's right. Raised platforms with steps had been installed so that he and Shiner could sit comfortably at the table. Two long tables extended down the hall from the high table to accommodate the assembled Etin nobles and, in the centre, coals burned in a great open hearth. The atmosphere was one of great jollity, though Snorri noticed many curious glances cast in his direction, which made him feel rather uneasy. Eventually, the King rapped thrice on the table and the hall fell silent. He stood and the assembled guests, Snorri and Shiner included, stood likewise. Holding a large horn in his right hand, the King addressed the throng.
"Nobles! Honoured guests! Greetings and welcome!"
Shouts of 'Greetings, your Majesty!' and 'Hail the King' resounded, echoing so loudly from the vaulted ceiling that Snorri's ears rang.
"Doubtless you have noticed", the King continued, "that we have two especially honoured guests with us tonight. The first you are well familiar with – Orvandil!"
There were cries of 'Hurrah!', and Shiner raised a hand in acknowledgement.
"The other is his companion, Snorri Sturluson, lately of Midgard."
The hubbub was stilled considerably, except for a few polite shouts of 'Hail Snorri!' and 'Welcome!', and the King resumed his speech.
"I say *lately* of Midgard, but he had quite a journey before he finally arrived here: a journey lasting over four hundred years. However, he wasn't dragging his feet; he had many adventures on the way, and even saved our friend Orvandil from death."
This last statement raised an enormous cheer, and the Giants rapped with their knuckles on the table to express their approval.
"Those of you familiar with the name of Snorri Sturluson", the King went on, "will no doubt know that he collected a lot of lore and

wrote it down. Some of it was about us, and let us say that not all of it was flattering."
Snorri blushed.
"But he has come here for the completion of his education about the Nine Worlds. Our realm has been left until last – the cherry on the cake, as it were – so I bid you all give him your best and kindest welcome. Now, raise your horns and cups: to Orvandil and Snorri!" The Etins enthusiastically took up the toast and sat again, some of them rubbing their stomachs and looking around to see whether food was on the way.

The first course was rapidly served, and consisted of oxtail soup and large hunks of brown bread. Most of the Etins drank straight from the bowl, but a few followed the example of the King and Queen and sipped delicately using unfamiliar spoons. Clearly, Snorri thought, a revolution in manners was underway. He tried to engage the King in small talk, but only obtained grunts in reply; the King believed in eating and in good conversation, but not both at the same time. Finally, the King laid his spoon on his empty bowl, gave a small belch, and showed that he had listened to Snorri's every word.
"Orvandil popular here? Yes, of course he is. Capital fellow. And a very wise counsellor when the occasion demands."
Snorri hesitated, seeking to frame his question tactfully.
"I had thought, Sire, that there might be some resentment. In my tales, I told of how Skírnir – I mean Orvandil – courted Gerd on Frey's behalf. He offered her many gifts, which she refused, and he ultimately resorted to compulsion with the threat of baneful magic."
The King took a swig of ale and laughed.
"Ah yes, Gerd. Bless her heart, but she was always a frosty bitch. Nine suitors she had already turned down, and her father, Gymir, despaired of her. She was beautiful, but a shrew, always nagging at him to make more of himself, though he was already old. He feared that he would be stuck with her forever. Then along came Orvandil,

and gave her the talking-to that she so thoroughly deserved. He did us a favour."

Snorri nodded and picked at some crumbs of bread.

"I heard she has returned to Etin-home", he said. The King sighed. "That's true, but she didn't go back to her father. She and Skadi – another cold, humourless one, also married to a Wane – took a liking to each other. Some say it's an unnatural relationship. Anyway, they settled in the high mountains and spend their days skiing together, and their nights… well, it doesn't matter. We are well rid of both of them, and those Vanir, father and son, must be suckers for punishment to make the same mistake twice! Fatal attraction of opposites, if you ask me."

Snorri had more questions, but now the main course was being served. He was offered the choice of an entire side of beef or a boar's head, the servants being unused to serving anything less. He thanked them and used his knife to carve off half a plateful of beef. Next came peas and unfamiliar potatoes, baked and served in their skins.

"What are these?", he enquired with furrowed brow as he poked despondently with his knife at the irregular, brown objects. A familiar voice spoke from behind his shoulder.

"They are called potatoes, Sir", said Laukrún. "Please forgive me that I could not be here earlier; I was engaged in other duties. They are the fruit of the earth, and good to eat. May I suggest that you tackle them – and the rest of your meal – with this tool, in conjunction with your knife?" He pointed toward the fork that lay to the left of the plate and, with the utmost discretion, coached him in its use. Snorri thanked him and tucked into the beef and vegetables, washing them down with sips of ale. The King, who had already cleared his plate, nudged him.

"Master Snorri, you are hardly drinking! Let us drink a decent toast – drink it down in one, so that your horn may be filled again. To eternal friendship!"

The King raised his horn, knocked it against Snorri's, and drank deeply. Snorri looked at his own small horn. It looked as though it might hold a pint, so he raised it, echoed "To eternal friendship!", drank until he thought to have emptied the horn, and put it down. The horn was still full, and he laughed.

"Sire, I am not Thor", he said with a smile, and the King chuckled.

"No, you are not, but you are a good drinker for a small mortal. Now, I assume you have many questions, so let me have them before the next course arrives. And don't forget to drink: it's the drinking that makes the feast!"

Taking another swig of ale, Snorri wondered where to start. He had so many questions about this blithe and hospitable race, who were turning out to be quite the opposite of the brutish creatures he had expected. He decided to begin with the simplest, a matter that had intrigued him since his arrival in Etin-home.

"How do you manage to get bigger or smaller when you want? I saw it a couple of times on my way to this city, though not since I arrived here. It must be some powerful kind of magic."

"Not magic", the King replied. "We Etins, unlike the Aesir, are not big on magic. It's just a matter of physics; we're good at that. Engineering too: you will remember how one of us, with only his stallion to help, built the walls of Asgard."

"Fizz-icks?", said Snorri quizzically, stumbling over the unfamiliar word.

"Aye, lad", the King replied. "You'll of course be aware of mass-energy equivalence; mass is just a different expression of energy, and vice-versa. It can be expressed in these equations."

The King dipped his finger into his ale, and traced a complex series of characters and wiggles on the table, none of which meant anything to Snorri. Seeing his baffled expression, the King patiently continued.

"What it comes down to is that we have the ability to shed or acquire mass at will, though it is transferred in the form of energy. When those hooligans had stopped trying to frighten you this morning, and became smaller, did you notice anything else?"

Snorri cast his mind back to the confrontation, the elder's admonishment, and the guilty transformation of the boisterous young giants, and then it hit him.

"Yes!", he said, "I remember that the air, and even the ground beneath my feet, got a lot warmer when they shrank!"

"There you go then", said the King, "all that mass had to go somewhere, so they shed it as heat energy. Fortunately, most of it went into the earth and melted some rocks deep below the surface, otherwise you and your friend would have been fried. The opposite happens too, when we want to get bigger. Have you ever heard the term 'frost giant'?"

Here, Snorri was on more familiar ground, and said that all the people of the north had heard of those. The King nodded.

"So let's imagine that one of us enters your little world, what you call Midgard. He's just normal size – about twenty feet or so in height – but then something threatens him, and he needs to get a lot bigger in a hurry. He draws in energy from the earth and from the air, and turns it into mass. Everything around him freezes, and the living things die of cold. Of course, there are some Etins – bad Etins, just as there are bad humans and cruel Gods – who do that kind of thing for the fun of it, but we don't encourage that kind of behaviour any more."

Snorri vaguely understood, and mentally filed it under the heading of 'Advanced Etin Magic' for further investigation. He picked at his meat and took another draught of ale from the self-replenishing horn. The ale was fruity and refreshing, and, unlike any other ale he had ever drunk, it did not dull his senses. He felt he could become pleasantly accustomed to it, and took another gulp. The King also drank, and continued his explanation.

"Changing size comes at a price. We don't like doing it. It makes us feel giddy and nauseous. That's why you don't see us doing it here in the city. It's also inconvenient to deal with when facing architecture of fixed proportions, if you see what I mean."

Snorri could appreciate that; it could certainly result in a lot of bumped heads and inconveniently narrow doorways. But there was something else that the King had said; it nagged at his mind, then came back to him.

"You say that you don't encourage that kind of behaviour any more. I heard that earlier today from the Giant who was on guard duty. He said something like 'we have a new boss, and we are not to go around making people frightened'."

The King sat back, smiled, and stretched his legs.

"That must have been young Fornrugg. Was he asleep when you found him?"

Snorri blushed, remembering Fornrugg's words and not wishing to get him into trouble, but the King waved a hand in casual dismissal of the matter.

"Fornrugg's a good lad, but not the sharpest knife in the drawer. He's also as lazy as they come. Truth to tell, we hardly need a guard at our border these days, so few are our visitors, but he volunteers for the duty to get out of doing chores for his mother. Then he sleeps and, as all Etins do when sleeping, enters the dream-time, the blessed condition of things before the Flood." The King's eyes, for a second, became misty.

Before the Flood! The words hit Snorri like a hammer. Was it possible that these Etins were Christians, and remembered Noah? Surely not! But then he remembered another flood – he had written about it himself – the outpouring of Ymir's blood as he was slain by Odin and his two brothers. The beneficial ale sharpened his mind and made it race, but his shoes were distracting him; they felt too tight on his feet, so he quietly kicked them off under the table.

"That... must have been a wonderful era", he ventured hesitantly. Do you remember anything of it? Fornrugg mentioned a 'new boss'." The King laughed again.

"Yes, I'm the new boss, and no, I don't remember anything of it, not in my waking hours at least. The old King passed away a thousand years ago, and I succeeded him. I was born relatively recently into the race of Giants, but I can remember you little folk scratting around in Midgard, making stone tools for yourselves. Odin and I reached an understanding soon after I came to the throne. He doesn't let his son Thor run amok and beat up my people, and I don't let my people intimidate the folk of Midgard. Simple. He says the Christians are our common enemy, and I can see the sense of that. He's up to something, the cunning old bugger, and says he has a plan that will benefit Aesir and Etins alike. You can never trust him entirely, but I'm willing to play along until the plan becomes clear. Sometimes you need to use cunning; he is good at that, and I am not."

The next course was served, consisting of fresh fruits, nuts and berries with honey and cream. They were as delicious as they looked, and Snorri surprised himself by finishing his bowl in a minute. With a sigh of satisfaction, he undid the top button of his trousers where it had begun to pinch at the waist, then stretched his arms and flexed his shoulders. There came a pop of breaking threads as he did so. The King was speaking to him again.
"Now then, Snorri, it is your turn to give a toast. Something to the whole assembly, eh?" Then, still seated, he rapped again on the table for silence, and the feasting giants stopped their conversations and looked up from their bowls.
"Nobles", said the King, our guest Snorri wishes to propose a toast!" Snorri stood, horn in hand. He supposed that he ought to feel embarrassed at being put on the spot thus, but he did not. On the contrary, he felt confident and even powerful. There was a loud ripping noise as he raised his horn in salute, and his tunic tore from wrist to waist and hung loosely from his right shoulder.
"Your Majesties! Etin Nobles!", he shouted with a ringing voice, "I thank you for this tremendous welcome. To friendship and to Jötunheim!"
"To friendship and to Jötunheim!", the Giants delightedly replied, and Snorri drank another two pints from his horn. As he did so, the stitches broke on the remainder of his shirt and tunic so that it fell down about his waist. This was just as well, for his trousers simultaneously burst apart and fell to his ankles. There was an enormous cheer, and Snorri looked to his right as a half-naked figure entered the central area around the hearth. It was Shiner, but he was ten feet tall at least. His body, previously lean and wiry, now rippled with bulging muscle, and he had gathered the flapping remnants of his clothes around him as a loin-cloth. With a broad grin, he pranced and leaped in a burlesque dance while the Giants cheered him on and began a rhythmic, drumming beat on the

tables. The rhythm coursed through Snorri's mind and body and, casting aside all restraint, he tore the shreds of his trousers from his ankles and joined Shiner in the dance. Twice they danced round the hearth, then linked elbows and danced in a circle, first one way and then the other. Finally, Shiner seized Snorri's left wrist, raised his arm high and shouted "FEE, FIE, FO, FUM!" There was a roar of applause from the Etins, who had tears running down their faces and were besides themselves with mirth. Some even fell from their seats and lay on the floor in helpless laughter. As Shiner slapped him on the back, Snorri realised that he, too, was close to Etin size. "That was fun, wasn't it?", said Shiner, panting a little. "They do this to me every time. I'm glad you joined in."

 They made their separate ways back to their places at the high table, where the platforms had been removed and bigger, sturdier chairs had been put in place. Smiling servants placed wide, woollen cloaks over their shoulders. As Snorri sat, the King wiped tears from his face and patted him on the shoulder.

"Well done, well done", he said, still laughing, "but tell me, what does 'fee, fie fo, fum' actually mean?"

"I don't know", Snorri replied, "I was hoping you would tell me. I never heard it until we met Fornrugg this morning", and the King roared again with laughter.

"We got it from some traveller who had read one of your Midgard stories. We thought it was funny, and now everyone uses it", he said.

Feeling very relaxed, Snorri drank more ale and smacked his lips. "This is quite some stuff", he said, "the berserkers of old would have given anything for a brew that makes you almost as big as a Giant."

"I doubt it", replied the King. "When you drink it, fighting is the last thing on your mind. It just makes you feel jolly and companionable. Of course, it does have that hilarious side-effect for humans, as Orvandil found out long ago."

Yes, thought Snorri; jolly and companionable: that was a good description for these Etin-folk. He marvelled at how wrong he had been in his old writings. Suddenly, for no particular reason, he remembered the orb that the King had held when he first greeted them on their arrival.

"Your orb, Sire", he said, "part of your royal regalia. What do the symbols on it mean?" And he traced the orb and its symbols in the spilled ale on the table.

"Oh, that old thing!", the King replied. "Well, that Hagall-rune on the orb itself; it doesn't mean 'hail', it represents Yggdrasil, the creation of the Aesir and Vanir, the structure that Odin imposed on everything. The Thurs-rune on the flange, pointing at Yggdrasil, represents our desire to smash the structure and abolish it."

Snorri caught his breath and stared.

"Is that what you really want? To destroy Yggdrasil and everything it encompasses?"

"No, of course not", the King replied, "not these days, anyway. It's an old bauble – perhaps tens of thousands of years old – that I inherited. Our ancestors in the distant past wished what it represents, hoping to restore the old way of things, but it was a vain hope. The Norns decreed that things should be as they are, and we have come to accept that. We, too, have a place in Yggdrasil, and it's not a bad system."

Snorri nodded.

"So you don't hate or resent Odin and the Aesir?"

"Ha!", the King snorted, "we did at first. We used to fight each other and play tricks on each other, seeking to gain the upper hand. There were even murders, especially by that lout Thor, Odin's bully-boy. He's a bit warped, if you ask me, and resents the fact that he's more than half Etin himself. But in the end, they matched our might with their magic, and we realised that it wasn't getting us anywhere. We are all related, after all: Odin himself is half-Etin by birth. We struck an accord, and now everything is in balance, and we like it that way. So no, we don't hate or resent them, but we don't fully trust them either."

He leaned closer to Snorri and spoke in a confidential tone.

"Listen, my lad. Never hate. Hate is like venom. You store it up to spit at an enemy, but it will eat you up from the inside and destroy you as well."

The King turned to speak to the Queen and respond to a humorous quip. The Queen was giggling, and he suspected she might be flirting with Shiner, or Orvandil as he knew him. Snorri, in the meantime, stared moodily into his horn and thought about the folk-tales he had been raised on; tales in which Giants had come striding down from the snow-clad peaks to terrorise farmers and gobble up their livestock. Cultured though his hosts had turned out to be, he almost felt sorry that those tales were not true, would not be true, had perhaps never been true. The thought saddened him. The King, satisfied that he had forestalled any flirtation, turned back to him.

"Why so glum, Snorri? Drink up! Ale is for drinking, not for looking at. The entertainment is about to start, so if you have any more questions, you had better ask them quickly."

Snorri forced himself to smile.

"Do you, the Etins I mean, ever visit Midgard now?"

The King's eyes opened wide in surprise.

"Visit Midgard? Why, of course we do! Not in the form that you see us in now, but we come to your Earth every autumn and winter as the gale's blast and the withering frost. We tear down that which cannot be sustained and purge the Earth of its overgrowth. We are the death-watch beetle in your rafters, and the worm in your coffin. We are destruction and the hand of time. And we are very, very necessary."

Then various instruments struck up a tune, the assembled Etins began to dance and sing, and no more questions were possible.

# Chapter 16 - Hrokkvir

The next morning, Snorri opened one eye and saw that Laukrún was quietly laying out the necessaries for his morning wash on the dressing table. He sat up, and Laukrún half-turned and spoke over his shoulder.
"Good morning, Sir! I trust you slept well?"
Snorri twisted his neck to the left and then the right, blinking the sleep from his eyes. To his surprise, he had not the slightest trace of a hangover, though he could not remember going to bed. He felt pleasantly rested and, moreover, noticed that he was back to his normal size.
"Thank you, Laukrún", he said, "as a matter of fact, I feel quite wonderful. I cannot remember the end of the feast, though. How did I get to bed?"
Laukrún smiled.
"You danced, Sir, and you drank more ale, then you fell asleep in your chair. Two Etins carried you to your bed, for you were too large for me to carry." He saw the look of embarrassment on Snorri's face and continued.
"Please don't worry, Sir. They don't consider a feast successful unless some of the guests fall asleep towards the end. Your friend Orvandil also fell asleep, on the dance floor, as did several of the Etins."
He bowed, and left to collect Snorri's breakfast. An hour later, Snorri was washed and dressed, and he wiped the last crumbs from his lips. He had found his own clothes hanging neatly on a rack at the end of the bed, and noticed that they had been washed and pressed. He smiled at the realisation that the old, cast-off clothes of the previous evening had been laid out for him in full knowledge of the effect that the ale would have. There came a loud knock at the door, and Shiner entered before he could even say 'Come in'. He looked excited, and his words came in a rush.
"Morning, old fellow. Finished your breakfast? Yes? Good! Now, get your coat and hat quickly; it seems that a guided tour has been arranged for us."

Together, they made their way to the atrium that lay in the middle of the citadel. It was a pleasant place, filled with birdsong and the sound of splashing water from a central fountain. The King was waiting for them, in conversation with the bizarrely-dressed shaman whom Snorri had glimpsed the day before. As Shiner and Snorri stepped into the light, the King turned to face them.

"Ah, Orvandil and Snorri! Good to see you. I trust you enjoyed our feast, hmm? I would like you to meet Hrokkvir, our chief shaman. He is to be your guide today, and he will fill you in on matters that we didn't get a chance to discuss yesterday evening."

The shaman acknowledged with a slight bow, his dark eyes boring deep into Snorri's own as though he were gauging him and measuring his soul. It made Snorri feel naked and uncomfortable, and it was only with effort that he focused again on what the King was saying.

"It has been a pleasure to meet you, Snorri, and I hope you will take away a good account of Etin-home. Unfortunately, I must attend to other matters and will not be around to see you off on the rest of your journey, so let us say our goodbyes now."

He extended a large hand, and Snorri took two fingers of it and shook them with bowed head. Then he raised his head to look directly at the King.

"Your Majesty", he said, "it has been a great pleasure to visit you and your realm. I thank you for all your hospitality, and for correcting the mistaken impression that I had collected about your people. I will strive to paint a fairer picture when next I write."

The King's eyes shone.

"Oh, it wasn't entirely mistaken, Master Snorri. Autumn's blast and winter's frost, remember? And now I must be off."

He strode away to one of the many doorways that lined the atrium, calling over his shoulder

"And Orvandil, it was good to see you too. Don't be a stranger! Don't let another six hundred years pass before we see you again."

Then he was gone, and they were left in the company of the shaman Hrokkvir, who simply said "Please follow me, gentlemen" and shambled away, bones clacking and feathers rustling.

He walked slowly, so that they might more easily keep up with him, through several corridors and up a couple of staircases. At the top of the second staircase, he paused to allow them to catch up, for the treads of the stairs were twice or three times the normal height for humans. Then he was off again, walking towards a door at the end of yet another corridor as Snorri and Shiner puffed after him. Hrokkvir paused at the door and pushed it open.
"Gentlemen", he announced, "the library of Etin-home's royal palace."
Snorri gasped. He saw a vast hall with shelf after towering shelf of books, and hundreds of pigeon-holes in which scrolls resided. Light from a tall window of stained glass shone down on their bindings. He had never considered that such a thing could exist. In his last time as a mortal human – how long ago had it been now? – a man had been rich in literature if he possessed a half-dozen books and scrolls. Most knowledge had still been passed on orally. Now his knees grew weak, and he literally staggered. Even Shiner stood in amazement at such a wealth of accumulated knowledge, for he had never been treated before to a visit to this library. They stumbled forward together, craning their necks this way and that, trying to read the titles on the spines of the books. Hrokkvir watched them, and only the closest and most familiar of his many apprentices would have noticed the slight smile on his lips. Snorri's eyes rolled, and he clutched his chest in an attempt to still the hyperventilation. "Oh... oh!", he gasped, "I shall need years – *years!* – to study all this!"
Hrokkvir remained impassive, concealing his amusement.
"I am afraid we do not have years", he said, "nor even a full day. Few who are not of the Etin-kind are even allowed to view the treasure of wisdom that we keep, so consider yourselves privileged. If it is any consolation, much of the collection is taken up by the biographies of every significant Etin who ever lived. Dull stuff, most of it. I have brought you here to inspect one particular volume, so that you may learn something of our history."
He led Snorri and Shiner along the central aisle to a tall lectern that stood directly under the high, stained-glass window. On the lectern,

glinting in the light, lay a leather-bound tome with brass fittings, its dimensions appropriately gigantic. When they reached the foot of the lectern, Hrokkvir gave a slight grunt of impatience, then brought over a wheeled step-ladder for the benefit of his small guests. Without asking, he unceremoniously picked up first Shiner and then Snorri, and deposited them on a step from which they could properly view the tome.

"This", said Hrokkvir, "is the Jötnarbók, the history of the Etin-kind, part of our sacred heritage."

He opened the cover, and it fell to the left with a deep, heavy thud. "The first pages, as you can see, are very old, faded and delicate. They were written on ox-hide thousands of years ago, but even these do not represent our first written records; those are carved in stone, and are kept in a repository elsewhere in the library. However, their contents have been transcribed onto vellum for more convenient reading."

He flipped forward, carefully turning the ancient pages. To Snorri's disappointment, they were all written in Etin-runes, and in the Old Etin language. He could not read them, but the illustrations were beautiful. Slowly, Hrokkvir turned the pages, and Snorri saw what could only be a creation scene depicting Ginnungagap, the yawning void, flanked by the fiery world of Muspelsheim and the icy world of Niflheim, all executed in red, yellow and black ink. Snorri shuddered involuntarily at his own memories of Niflheim. The pages turned again, and he saw Ymir, the first giant, and his many offspring. Then came the murder of Ymir by the brothers Odin, Vili and Vé, Etins drowning as oceans of blood poured forth, and the saving of Bergelmir and his kin. All the time, Hrokkvir gave a running commentary, summarising the written accounts. There followed scenes of exclusion, resentment and war, in which a red-bearded, hammer-wielding figure featured prominently: that could only be Thor. As Hrokkvir continued to turn the pages, exposing more peaceful episodes in the Etins' history, Snorri thought back to his conversation with the King, and a question that still remained unanswered.

"I was told that in sleep you dream of the old times, before the slaying of Ymir. What was it like then? Our lore relates that it was noisy and chaotic, and that Odin and his brothers killed Ymir because they couldn't stand it any longer. What is the truth of it?" Again, the dark, piercing eyes bored into his soul as Hrokkvir considered his answer.

"I was not there", he replied. "None who were there in the beginning still live, except Odin. But it is true that we return to that time every night, when we sleep, and it was beautiful. It was neither noisy nor chaotic, but Odin and his brothers were not, could not be content. We sang, but they wanted a different tune, and it had to be *their* tune, so that they could shape things according to their will. They were mutants, having inherited a dangerous strain from their grandfather, Buri – nobody really knows where he came from – and we failed to realise the danger until it was too late, so busy were we with the simple joy of existence."

Snorri was about to ask another question, but Shiner spoke first. "You say that Odin is the only one who was there before Ymir's death, and still lives. How can that be?"

"I do not know the secret of his longevity", replied Hrokkvir. Idunn's apples are perhaps part of the answer, but they came later. Whatever his secret, I think he must bear it like a curse since he discovered it. All living things cling to life, and evade death insofar as possible. It is in their nature. Give them the secret of eternal life, and they will hang on forever, unless killed. But life eventually becomes tedious, as I know all too well, having lived through many ages. Perhaps that is why Odin secretly desires Ragnarök and the release it will bring."

He looked up at the high window, gauging the position of the sun, then closed the massive book.

"It is already noon, and there is still much to do and see", he said, and he lifted Snorri and Shiner from their perches on the ladder and lowered them back to the floor.

From the library they made their way to the citadel's forecourt, where the King had received them the previous day. Now the place was all but deserted, and it appeared that the inhabitants of the city must all be at their work, or perhaps having lunch. Despite the sunshine, the day was cold, and a chill wind blew dust across the flagstones in small eddies. Shiner shivered briefly. Galdrafaxi was there, already saddled and bridled, and the bags containing their possessions were attached to the saddle. Shiner put on his cloak, and Snorri donned the voluminous, brown coat that Gróa had given him. They mounted up and, without a word, Hrokkvir set off through the quiet streets towards the rear gate, a smaller portal than the great gateway by which they had entered. The gatekeeper, clearly in awe of Hrokkvir, gave a small wave and opened the gate, and then they were out in the open countryside. Outside the walls, a group of Etins appeared to be engaged in some kind of work, shifting heavy stones under the watchful eye of an overseer. Snorri watched them and was puzzled to see that their work made no practical sense; they were simply passing the stones in a circle, clockwise. One would pick up a boulder at his feet, lift it, and place it before the feet of the Etin to his left, and then repeat the action with a different boulder. He was about to comment when Shiner already supplied the answer.

"They are the young Etins who tried to frighten us yesterday. This must be their punishment."

Not too harsh a punishment, Snorri thought. The Giants were not even sweating, and one, seeing them, gave a cheery wave, which earned a scowl and a rebuke from the overseer. Snorri waved back anyway to show that there were no ill feelings. With an easy, swinging stride, Hrokkvir followed a sandy path that crossed a broad heath, a bronze kettle, an iron tripod and other items dangling and jangling at his waist. On a rope over his shoulder, he carried a faggot of kindling. Ancient he might be, but he maintained such a pace that Galdrafaxi had to trot to keep up. Five miles from the city, they approached a series of low hillocks and, as they drew level, Snorri saw that they formed a circle with one larger hill in the middle. Hrokkvir halted and turned to face them, pointing towards the features with a sweep of his arm.

"The barrow-mounds of our ancestors", he announced. "One day, I shall lie with them, perhaps as part of a new, outer ring."
He studied the barrows in pensive silence for a few moments before continuing.
"Some of those lying here – just a few – knew the old times. Under the big one in the middle lie Bergelmir and his wife. They died long ago, too soon even to see the first humans, but still at an immense age. We Etins are not immortal, but we live a very long time by your reckoning. I have seen stars being born, and I have seen the same stars explode in their death-throes. We are the very forces of nature."
Then, without further explanation, he was off again, and the two companions trotted after him. Looking back, Shiner thought he saw stealthy movement among the barrows and squinted against the sun, shielding his eyes with his hand. Snorri followed his gaze.
"What is it?", he asked.
"I don't know", Shiner replied. "It may only have been a cloud shadow, but my gut tells me that we are being followed."
Digging his heels into Galdrafaxi's flanks, he urged the horse forward at a faster pace until they rode level with Hrokkvir.
"Where are we going, exactly?", called Shiner, his head level with the shaman's belt. Without breaking his stride, Hrokkvir replied.
"We are bound for Bergelmir's Point, a special and very sacred place. Have you heard of it?"
"No", Shiner admitted. "What makes it so special?"
"It is the site where Bergelmir and his family landed at this place, this world, which was to become Etin-home", said Hrokkvir, "a site where some of the old magic lingers and one can get a better view of the whole-all."

They rode on, Hrokkvir still striding in the lead along a way that was effectively ceasing to exist, for now there was no vegetation to distinguish between heath and path. Gradually, the sun became dimmer, as though an eclipse were taking place, and bird-song ceased. The sky grew darker and, one by one, stars appeared. Finally, under the faintest light, they reached a narrow promontory that jutted out into space. There, Hrokkvir stopped and laid down the bundle of kindling that he had carried for so many miles. He fumbled at his belt, releasing the kettle and the tripod to fall with a clang to the ground. Snorri dismounted and walked to the edge of the headland. Above, around and below him, stars blazed, the Milky Way forming a dazzling chain that bisected the sky and gave enough light to see by. His contemplation was interrupted by the sound of steel striking flint, and Hrokkvir's powerful exhalations as he blew on the assembly of birch bark and small twigs that were cupped in his palms. Flaming light sprang up, impeding his night vision, and he felt cheated, but the shaman only added to the fire and made it blaze more brightly. He watched as Hrokkvir assembled the tripod, hung the kettle over it, and poured water from a leather bottle. Satisfied, with the bulk of the kindling lying next to the fire, Hrokkvir sat cross-legged.

"It is a fine view, Master Snorri, do you not agree?", he said.
Snorri turned his back to the fire and allowed his pupils to expand again. With nothing to reflect the firelight, he could soon see the heavenly vista again in all its magnificence. It was much the way that it had been on their flight through Midgard, but here it seemed to hold more meaning, some... how to define it? ... some more profound history.

"Would you see more?", came Hrokkvir's voice again. "You have wondered what it was like in the old time, the Etin-time, before the Flood. I can show you that. I can show you what Etins see in their dreams, when they return to the Ginnung."

He flung another log on the fire, and the water in the kettle began to seethe. Snorri stared at the fire, then looked up into the brown pools of Hrokkvir's eyes, which held reflections of the flames.

"I would like that very much he said."
The shaman took an oilskin-covered package from the pouch at his side. It looked tiny in the large fingers, but Shiner recognised it as the package that Odin had entrusted to him, and he felt a spasm of foreboding. Hrokkvir was taking the dried leaves from their covering and scattering them on the boiling water. Shiner turned to Snorri and seized his upper arm.

"Snorri, I have a bad feeling about this", he hissed. "I have felt uneasy since we woke up this morning, and the feeling has stayed with me all day. You don't have to do this."

The steam from the quickening brew wafted into Snorri's nostrils, and he welcomed it. It made him feel peaceful. He placed his hand on Shiner's and looked into his face.

"Don't worry, my friend", he said, "I really want to see this. If I don't, I will always wonder what I missed."

Hrokkvir, with a gesture, bade Snorri sit down on the ground next to him, and used a ladle to pour the tea into two cups. He placed one before Snorri, the other at his own feet.

"Let it cool", he said, "and, in the meantime, enjoy the stars."

Shiner sat behind them, agitated. There was Odin's hand in this, and he well knew not to trust the motivations of that old manipulator. From the corner of his eye, he detected movement. Yes, there it was again! He silently rose and drew his seax from its sheath, but found himself looking into Hrokkvir's forbidding eyes. The shaman moved his hand, palm downwards, insisting that he should sit down again and not interfere. Reluctantly, he complied.

When the brew had cooled sufficiently, Hrokkvir turned to Snorri.

"It is time", he said, "let us drink."

And they both drained the contents of their cups. Snorri winced at the bitterness of the tea and felt its warmth course down into his stomach. He waited for a while. Nothing seemed to be happening until a wave of nausea passed through him and he vomited onto the ground before him. Hrokkvir also vomited, and then they both stood and took a couple of paces forward together, looking out across the starry void.

"That's the part I don't like, the vomiting", Hrokkvir said with a smile, and nodded back towards the fireplace. Snorri looked back and saw himself, still sitting on the ground, cross-legged and with closed eyes, next to a sleeping Hrokkvir. Shiner stood behind them, peering suspiciously into the kettle. He turned back to look at the void, but the stars were not in their former configurations. They had congregated together to form an enormous, glittering tree that filled the sky.

"Behold Yggdrasil", said Hrokkvir.
Snorri viewed the apparition with rapture. He extended an arm to touch it with his hand, and the outer leaves and branches tenderly twined around his fingers. Slowly, gently, he pushed deeper, up to his elbow, and touched the bole of the tree, feeling the pulsing flow of its sap and the brief, busy lives of a billion mortals.
Simultaneously, Yggdrasil embraced him, and they merged. His spine became the trunk, his legs the roots, his arms the spreading branches, and in a blinding flash he saw and experienced everything, everywhere, all at once. The vision came in the form of a rapid series of images, accompanied by an ecstatic paean of praise to life itself. Sun and moon raced across the sky; seasons and ages passed in rapid succession; plants, animals, humans and even gods were born, lived, reproduced and died, their remains sinking and becoming fertile soil for new life. Growth, destruction, and everything that Men call 'good' and 'evil' were perfectly balanced. Snorri experienced a surge of supreme bliss as his consciousness extended to every root, branch, twig and leaf of his being. Then, just as he thought that there could be nothing more to know, the connections detached as gently as they had been made, and Yggdrasil released him, slowly withdrawing until they stood as separate entities once more.
"Would you know more?", whispered Hrokkvir's voice, and the stars of Yggdrasil began to blink out, disappearing until only a few remained. Bark fell from the roots, bole and branches, exposing a stark, angular structure made of steel, concrete and glass. Lights still remained, but they were organised into regular matrices along the rectilinear bole and branches. At junctions along the bole and at the terminations of the branches, cuboid structures bulged: the Nine Worlds, as conceived by some soulless architect. Life, too, remained, but it moved in regimented fashion; up, down, and horizontally. Conflict was eliminated, and also joy. Functionality ruled.
Behind the horrified Snorri came the whispering voice again.
"This is how they initially conceived it. This is how we perceived it. Were it not for the input of the Vanir, this is how it would have

been. They were born into paradise, but paradise was not orderly enough for them, so they tore it up and used its pieces to construct their own project. See you now why we strove for aeons to destroy this, and return the whole-all to its primaeval state?"
"Show me that paradise, please", pleaded Snorri. "That is what I truly need to see."
For a moment – or was it an age? It was hard to tell now – there was only silence, and then the lights blinked out again, leaving only darkness. Gradually, the darkness was replaced by a diffuse light that had no source. Growing brighter, it came in waves of many colours, sweeping, flowing and shifting, surrounding Snorri. He looked back and saw that the promontory had disappeared; only he, Hrokkvir and the light existed. Then came the singing, almost inaudible at first, but rising in volume. It was more beautiful and harmonious than any earthly choir, and Snorri felt himself float on the light and the music. Though he had not conceived it possible, an even greater sense of bliss overcame him, a feeling of perfect love. He wanted only for the separation to end, and to be part of the glory around him. Hrokkvir watched as Snorri began to spread and merge with the light, dancing, flowing and mingling with each successive wave until it was impossible to distinguish his individual shape. When he was satisfied that Snorri had utterly disintegrated, he regretfully pulled himself back from the scene and returned to his physical body at the fireside.

The natural toxins in the tea, administered in a dose that an Etin could absorb without harm but was fatal to a human, coursed through Snorri's system, quietly shutting down one organ after another until they reached his heart and brain, and, with a beatific smile on his face, Snorri died. Shiner, who had waited for an anxious hour, quelling his desire to interfere, saw him fall sideways and rushed to him. Placing a hand on his chest, he felt for a pulse, but there was only the stillness of death.
"You've killed him!", Shiner yelled, tears coursing down his face. Hrokkvir opened his eyes, yawned and stretched.

"No, my friend", he replied. "Snorri died centuries ago, and has been living on borrowed time at the decree of Odin. Do not be sad; he will live again, if I interpreted the message aright."

At the edge of the flickering firelight, shadows gathered themselves into a recognisable form, and Fundinn walked quickly towards Snorri's prostrate body. With an experienced eye, he examined his misty ghost, which still sat by the fire. Shiner watched as he laid out his tool-roll and took a glass rod and a small vial.

"Yes, there we go; memories all nicely intact and preserved, soul where it ought to be", Fundinn muttered to himself as he wound the memory-skeins onto the rod and placed them into the vial. "Quite a lot of 'em, too", he chuckled, "more than your average mortal."

"So it was you following us", said Shiner dully, still in shock.

"Oh yes", replied Fundinn, "we dwarfs can be exceedingly stealthy when the situation calls for it. Allfather brought me here on Sleipnir a day ago and dropped me off. Have you got any food? I didn't think to bring any."

He returned to his work, bringing out a long pair of tweezers and another vial.

"Here, where's his cognition? I can't find it!"

Hrokkvir, who had been watching the procedure with interest, spoke up.

"His cognition is out there... everywhere", he said with a vague wave of his arm. "Don't worry, it will come back. They always do when there is unfinished business, but it may take some time. When it does, I will collect it and send it on to you. I will see that the body is buried in our barrow-ring; he has no further use for it."

Together, Shiner and Fundinn stood over the corpse. Suddenly, out of the darkness, a breeze sprang up, and Snorri's ghost disappeared on it like so much smoke. Released, the shining orb of his soul slowly drifted away, Hel-bound. Shiner sighed, then gave a whistle to summon Galdrafaxi.

"Come on, Fundinn", he said, "we have a soul to follow. Since he is to live again, I wish to help select a decent body for him."

And together they rode, following the rapidly receding soul.

**THE END**

Printed in Great Britain
by Amazon